Caught Up in the Life

Robert Baptiste

Lock Down Publications and Ca$h
Presents

Caught Up in the Life

A Novel by *Robert Baptiste*

Robert Baptiste

Lock Down Publications
P.O. Box 870494
Mesquite, Tx 75187

Visit our website @
www.lockdownpublications.com

Copyright 2020 Robert Baptiste
Caught Up in the Life

First Edition February 2020
Printed in the United States of America

Lock Down Publications
Like our page on Facebook: Lock Down Publications @
www.facebook.com/lockdownpublications.ldp
Cover design and layout by: **Dynasty Cover Me**
Book interior design by: **Shawn Walker**
Edited by: **Nika Michelle**

Stay Connected with Us!

Text **LOCKDOWN** to 22828 to stay up-to-date with new releases, sneak peaks, contests and more...

Thank you.

Submission Guideline.

Submit the first three chapters of your completed manuscript to ldpsubmissions@gmail.com, subject line: Your book's title. The manuscript must be in a .doc file and sent as an attachment. Document should be in Times New Roman, double spaced and in size 12 font. Also, provide your synopsis and full contact information. If sending multiple submissions, they must each be in a separate email.

Have a story but no way to send it electronically? You can still submit to LDP/Ca$h Presents. Send in the first three chapters, written or typed, of your completed manuscript to:

LDP: Submissions Dept
Po Box 870494
Mesquite, Tx 75187

DO NOT send original manuscript. Must be a duplicate.

Provide your synopsis and a cover letter containing your full contact information.

Thanks for considering LDP and Ca$h Presents.

To my mother Gail Baptiste, my girl Ke'shon Williams, RIP to my baby mother Katrina Cater, RIP to my wife, Lillian Perkins. And my favorite Sister in Law Mookie.

Robert Baptiste

Caught Up in the Life

Prologue

I pulled up to the gleaming white colonial mansion on the north side of Houston. It sat on what had to be fifty acres. As I got out of my car a bodyguard patted me down to check for guns and wires. He escorted me past a row of expensive Land Rovers, Porches, Ferraris and Bentleys into the house. As I waked in, I saw a huge floor inlaid with marble, crystal and expensive woods. It glowed under the lights.

My escort took me into a conference room. A huge mahogany table surrounded by black leather chairs dominated the room. Around the table, I saw people from all walks of life. They were black, white, Latino, men, women, old, and young. They all wore business suits and were in the same business: selling drugs for the cartel.

I sat at the table and put on my best fake smile as we waited for Deloso. It was quiet as shit. You could hear a rat piss on cotton. No lie, I was nervous as fuck. I had never been to something like this before.

Deloso, the head of the cartel, walked into the room carrying a wooden baseball bat. He was dressed in an all-black Armani suit. He stopped at the head of the table and stared at all of us. His bodyguards entered the room, blocking the doors behind them.

I got even more nervous. I didn't have a clue what was going on. It seemed as if a threat hung in the air. Everyone at the table seemed to grow apprehensive. It was visible on their faces and in their body language.

"Somebody isn't playin' fair," Deloso began as he walked around the table. He punctuated his steps by lightly hitting the bat against his hand. "Somebody has been talkin' to the Feds."

My heart dropped to my ass.

"Ya'll know what I do to people who talk to the Feds. And even worse, my money has been short. Remember, there's only two rules: don't fuck with my money and don't talk to the Feds.

He stopped behind my chair. Sweat poured from my armpits as my heart raced. I gripped my chair tight, preparing for the worst.

Suddenly, he cocked the bat back and slammed it into the head of the Mexican sitting to my left.

I thought I had shit myself. I know I farted.

I watched as blood gushed out of his head and all over me and Deloso. He lay on the table with his skull crushed, bits of brain and a sea of blood surrounding him. His eyes were still open, seeming to stare at me accusingly.

Deloso calmly continued to hit him in the head over and over, almost serenely. He stopped hitting him and looked around the room. "I hate pigs and thieves." Deloso called to a bodyguard, "Give Ms. B a gun. I need her to finish this pig."

I took the gun and shot him. I didn't have a choice. Besides, it was mercy. He couldn't live like that.

Deloso took the gun from me. Everyone at the table shot the corpse. See, now they couldn't tell which of us killed him. Plus, we'll all have blood on our hands.

"Get him out of here. I want his entire fuckin' family dead. All of them. Remember the message, people. Don't fuck with me, or you will end up like that motherfucker. Don't think any of you are untouchable. Mario worked with me for twenty years. We grew up together. Meeting is adjourned. Same time and place in a couple months." Deloso left the room.

Shakily, I got to my feet and went to my car thinking, *What the fuck have I gotten myself into? More importantly, what have I gotten my family into?*

Caught Up in the Life

Chapter 1

Shantell

Here I was running on a treadmill in our $1.5 million dollar house in East-over Drive in New Orleans East. We lived in one of the biggest subdivisions in the city. A lot of rich black people lived here including doctors, lawyers, congressmen and businesspeople who own successful companies. My husband was one of those people. He owned a construction company that earns fifty million in annual revenue.

That was why I was trying to keep my 5'3 thick, red frame in shape for my man. It was our tenth anniversary tonight. He'd been asking me for another threesome. I wasn't messed up about it. I looked at it this way. If I didn't do it, another bitch would. I'd be damned if I let some random bitch come in and take my man. I worked hard to get him the way I wanted him. I'd put up with too much bullshit to let a bitch take him from me. All the headaches and pain. All the hoes and cheating. All the nights staying up late worrying if he would be killed in the streets, costing my kids a father and me a husband.

So, I'd be fucked if I let that happen. I'd kill them both. I wouldn't mind doing life in prison behind it.

So, I did what I had to do to keep my man happy. I didn't mind a little girl on girl action every now and again. He was a good man, a good husband and a good father to our two kids. He took care of his family, making sure that we had everything we needed. We didn't want for anything. Our kids were getting a great education in the best private school in the city. I drove around in a Mercedes Benz G Wagon that costs $170,000. I carried $20,000 purses on my arm and wore the latest fashions from the hottest designers such as Louis Vuitton, Gucci, Prada, or whoever else I desired. Money was not a thing with Keith.

Keith used to sell drugs back in the day. When I got pregnant with our son, he started to slow down. When our daughter was born, he left the game completely and started being a good husband and father. He started a construction company. Now, it was one the biggest in the city. I was glad he got his shit together because my mother wanted me to leave his black ass altogether. She still didn't believe that he had changed. She didn't believe leopards can change their spots. She thought he was a womanizer, a hoe to be exact.

She blamed him for getting me pregnant, which caused me to drop out of college. I told her all the time it takes two to lay down and make a baby, but she didn't want to hear that shit. See, I was her only child. She still looked at me as her baby. I understood to a certain extent. When he used to fuck me over, I would run crying to her.

Keith never hit me. He just broke my heart a million fucking times. Like a stupid ass, I kept going back. Why? I couldn't even lie. That nigga could put it down in the bedroom and have a bitch out of her mind cuming back to back. I saw why those hoes would chase after him, and I was one of them. I broke the windows out of his car, cut his tires, and fought a lot of other hoes over him. So, I knew a little something about being stupid for a man when you were in love with him.

"Enough of that." I stepped off the treadmill and went to the bathroom to shower. I let the hot water flow over my body. It felt so good that I let two fingers slide between my legs. I rubbed on my already swollen clit, letting my other hand dance over my hard-erect nipples. I cum so hard my knees buckle. Recovering from my near swoon, I got out of the shower.

'Shit, I needed that,' I said to myself as I dried off.

I went to our bedroom and looked at myself naked in the full-length mirror at our bedside. It was the one I liked to watch myself in when we fucked. I kind of looked like Shantell Jackson who was dating the rapper Nelly. I had a round fat ass that I got from my mother and nice watermelon sized breasts.

I always checked my body to make sure nothing was out of place, or no lumps were on my breasts or any shit like that. You know, a bitch had to be careful nowadays. See, you have to know yourself.

One thing I knew was, if my titties started sagging, I'd be getting implants like those Hollywood bitches. You better believe that shit.

I turned around to check my legs, ass and hips for cellulite because that shit wasn't cute at all. If I ever looked like I'm getting that shit, it was time to go under the knife, and that's gospel. I did squats to keep my ass fat, round and firm just like he liked it. He loved to rub on it

12

after we made love or when we sat around and watched TV in the bedroom. I couldn't lie. That shit felt good, it put my ass to sleep. I was at a point where I could barely fall sleep if he wasn't rubbing on it. My ass was soft and smooth like a newborn baby's skin.

My thoughts were interrupted as my cell phone rang. I quickly picked it up off the charger. "Hello."

"Hey girl. We still on for tonight?" the sexy voice asked.

"Yeah. I need you to come at about eight."

"Okay, I got you."

"All right, I'll see you then."

"Bye." She hung up.

I looked at the clock and saw it was already 2:30 pm. It was almost time to pick up the kids from school. I put on a gray Sean John jogging suit and gray Air Maxs. I pulled my long black hair in a ponytail, grabbed my black Gucci purse and called my mother as I pulled out of my driveway. I was hoping she would watch the kids for me. I had something special planned for Keith.

"Hello," she answered her phone.

"Mom, I need you to do me a favor. Can you watch the kids tonight?

"Bring 'em over. I got you."

"Love you, mom."

"I know."

"Bye."

With all the shit she gave me for having kids, she loved them more than I did. She wanted them around her all the time. She spoiled their asses rotten. At her house, they could get away with murder. That was why they always wanted to go there. She let them do whatever they wanted.

I, on the other hand, didn't play that shit. Keith said I was too hard on them sometimes. Fuck that. I was not one of those mothers who let their kids talk to them any way they wanted. I'd get in their ass. *Homie don't play that.*

I pulled up to the school, and they were outside waiting on me. They jumped in the backseat as soon as I stopped.

13

"Mom? We going by grandmother Shelly's house?" Keith Jr. asked.

"Yes," I said smiling.

"Mom, I need my hair fixed," Kawaine said.

"Ask your grandmother to wash it, and I'll take you to see Aunt Jackie tomorrow."

"Okay," she replied.

"Now, y'all get your seatbelts on."

My phone rang. It was the love of my life, Keith. What attracted me to him in the first place was I thought he was a pro basketball player. He had a lot of ice on and drove a black Benz with dark tinted windows and chrome rims. The whole city knew who he was. They loved him, but at the same time they feared him. All the hoes in the city were on his dick.

I met him near my best friend Jackie's house in the projects. She was doing my hair back then too. I had heard a lot about him from the hoes getting their hair done. They were gossiping about him, telling how much money he had and how he was fucking bitches all over the city.

One day, I stepped my hot ass out of my car at Jackie's house to get my hair fixed. It was summer, and I had on some short, pink shorts that were riding all up in my ass and a matching T-shirt that was cut at the stomach to show off my diamond belly ring. I was definitely cute and fresh out of college on a break.

Keith was on the side of the building shooting dice with some of his homeboys. As I went up the stairs all the niggas were staring at me, but he was the only one that stepped up to me. He walked over wearing some black Polo jeans shorts with a white wife-beater, showing his ripped-up muscles. His white Polo shirt was draped over his shoulder with his white Polo tennis shoes looking fresh out of the box. A black gun was visible in the waist of his jeans. He stood about 6'4 with smooth, dark skin that made my pussy instantly get wet. It also helped that he favored D. Wade from the Miami Heat.

He introduced himself showing his pearl-white teeth. He smelled so good. Normally, I wouldn't give any play to a nigga like him, but the hoes talked about this nigga every time I came over there. So, curiosity got the best of me.

I should have run far away from this nigga as fast I could, but no. When he spoke to me with his raspy D.M.X. voice my pussy got even wetter. I was hooked from that point on, and a bitch gave the pussy up on the first night. We've been rocking strong for the last ten years now with a six-year old daughter and an eight- year- old son. I'm his ride - or- die bitch.

"Hey, baby," I greeted him as I smiled from ear to ear.

"What's up, Miss Lady? I'm calling to check on you. Just wanted to know how your day is going."

"It's been good. Especially now that I hear your voice. I just got the kids from school, and I'll drop them off at my mother's house tonight."

"Okay, Let's get it poppin' then. We going out tonight?"

"Yeah, I got you."

"Okay, I love you."

"Love you back."

"Tell the kids I love them."

"Kids, your father said he love y'all."

"We love you too, daddy."

We ended the call.

I loved my life. I had the best husband in the world and the smartest, cutest kids. That was because they get their looks from me and Keith. Plus, it didn't hurt that I was a hot thirty year old chick that could pass for a young twenty-five. I still gave those young hoes a run for their money.

I dropped the kids off at mother's house and drove over to Jackie's to get my hair, nails, and toes done. Afterward, I rushed home to cook Keith's favorite dinner of steak and stuffed baked potatoes. The clock said it was only six o' clock, so I still had time for a hot bath before Keith and a special guest arrived.

I jumped in the tub, luxuriating in the hot, steamy, bubble-filled bath. After washing up with some watermelon body wash, I got out of the tub and put on Keith's favorite watermelon Victoria's Secret lotion.

As I lit my strawberry scented candles, I heard the doorbell ring. It was only seven o' clock.

"Damn, she early," I said to myself as I walked to the door. I looked through the peephole to make sure it was her. The front gate didn't call to tell me. I had to talk to somebody about that.

A young woman was standing there in a long, black coat. I opened the door smiling at her. She smelled like wild cherries. "You early, huh?"

"Better early than late." She smiled as she walked in. "You smell good."

"Just got out the tub."

"Where you want me to put my coat?" She took off her coat and stood in front of me wearing only a blue thong with a matching bra and heels. This bitch was bad. Icy had a banging body like a stripper with caramel skin. She was 5'5, and thick in all the right places like government cheese. She had a long, red weave that hung down to her ass with pretty, hazel eyes. She was mixed with black and Spanish, reminding me of the rapper Nicki Minaj. I wasn't into women like I used to be. I hadn't thought about having a serious relationship with a woman in years, but damn! If she had caught me back in the day, I would have been her bitch.

"Damn, you fine," I told as I took her coat.

"Thank you. You look like you got a fine ass shape under that robe."

I untied my robe. I was wearing nothing underneath it. I let her check me out. I was glad I shaved my pussy. I turned around to let her see my fat ass.

"Dang. You got a banging body. Looks like you work out."

"I try to keep this thing tight and right.

"Look like you doing a good job to me."

I had met Icy on the internet. She'd hit me up on my Facebook page trying to get with me. I told her I was married and didn't get down without my husband. I met with her a couple of times for drinks. I asked if she wanted to get down with me and my husband in a threesome. She was with it. It helped that she was cute, thick and red with a big, fat ass like Keith liked.

16

She walked over and touched my breasts. My nipples were so hard it was a shame. She slid her hands down to my pussy. I was soaking wet. She had me so turned on.

She eased her finger inside my pussy and began to kiss me. I gripped her ass, pulling her close to me as we tongue kiss one another.

I heard Keith's keys jiggling in the door. Breaking off our kiss, I rushed her into the spare bedroom. "Stay here until I come get you."

"Okay, I got you."

I walked back to the living room, retying my robe. I walked up to Keith and hugged and kissed him. "Hey, baby. You home early."

"Yeah, I knew we were going out. So, I· took off early. Damn it smell good in here. I thought we were going to eat out."

"Change of plans. I thought we could stay home and get to know each other even better." I smiled as I took him by the hand to led him to the kitchen.

I left Keith eating at the table to check on Icy. "You straight?"

"I'm good."

"Just a few more minutes."

"Okay."

I went back to the kitchen to get Keith. "Come on, baby. Let's go take a bath," I suggested.

"Damn! Baby, you smell good. Looks like you took one already," he said kissing me.

"I did, but I want to show you how much I love you."

"Whatever you want," he panted.

We went to the bathroom, and he looked around at the scented candles and hot bubble bath.

"All this for me?" he asked.

"Shh, let me help you get out all them clothes."

I helped him into the tub and washed his body. Stroking his dick, I teased it while tongue kissing him.

"Finish up," I said as I walked out.

"Where you going?"

"Meet me in the bedroom."

I grabbed Icy and put her in the bedroom closet. "I'll give you a signal to come out."

"Okay."

I lay on the bed on my stomach naked with my ass in the air as I waited for Keith. He came in with a towel wrapped around his waist. Keith removed his towel as he walked toward me, exposing his erect nine-inch dick. I wasn't talking a slim nine. I was talking about a wide and thick nine that fills up a bitch's pussy walls.

"That's how we doing it tonight?" He stroked his dick while looking at my ass.

"Any way you want it." I crawled over to him and caressed his dick while sucking the head a little bit. "Hold on, baby. Let me blindfold you."

"What?"

"Come on. It's gonna be fun. I promise you."

"Damn! You on some real freaky shit tonight."

"I told you I had a few tricks up my sleeve."

I blindfolded him and helped him get in the bed. Then I signaled for Icy to come out of the closet. She walked over and climbed into bed with us. We began to suck his dick together. I sucked his balls while Icy worked on his dick.

"Damn, baby, your mouth all over me."

I took the blindfold off so he could see Icy sucking on his dick. After taking her thong off, I started eating her pussy from the back while she deep throated his dick like a porn star.

"Fuck! That feel so good," he moaned, watching her swallow his whole dick. He got up, put on a rubber and hit her from the back as I spread my legs, letting her eat me out. I grabbed her hair and grinded my pussy in her face, cuming all in her mouth. Icy mounted his dick and started riding him like a horse.

Keith took of the rubber and climbed on top of me. He put my legs on his shoulders and slid his dick inside me. He fucked me hard and deep as I dug my nails into his back.

"Fuck! I love you," I screamed cuming back to back while Icy sucked on my titties.

We both assumed the doggy-style position, letting him fuck both of us from behind. I watched sweat drip off his body as he hit her from the back. He looked so good that it turned me on even more.

He started to shake. We quickly turned around and let him shoot his cum all in our faces. He watched as Icy and I kissed, sharing his cum.

"Happy tenth anniversary, baby," I said as I kissed him.

"I love you," he replied.

"I love you back."

He sat back in the chair watching Icy and I sixty-nine each other until we climaxed back to back.

*   *   *

I woke up the next morning with a big ass smile on my face. I had never cum as much as I did the night before. Keith had joined us again. We fucked the shit out of him until he had to stop. That bitch Icy knew she could eat pussy right.

I looked at Keith's side of the bed, but he was already up. I put Icy's ass out earlier that morning after we finished. I didn't play that spending the night, waking up with me and my man shit. It was cool that we did what we did, but when it was all said and done, the bitch had to go.

I heard the shower running, got out of bed and strolled to the bathroom. I saw Keith's sexy body through the glass shower door. Thinking about how he put that dick on me last night made me want some more. Thinking about him fucking the shit out of Icy turned me on even more. I opened the shower door studying him from head to toe. This man was a god.

"Can I join you?" I asked with a seductive leer.

"Of course." He smiled.

I climbed in and kissed him passionately. "How you like your surprise?"

"I loved it, but I love you most."

"I love you back."

Keith picked me up and inserted his dick inside my tightness. I wrapped my legs around him as he bounced me up and down on his dick. I encircled him in my arms and bit his shoulder gently, enjoying simultaneous waves of pleasure and pain at the same time. I cum all over his dick. He put me down, and I bent over, grabbing the shower nozzles as he slammed his dick in and out of my wet pussy. He grabbed my ass cheeks tightly, shaking, releasing all his hot nut in me.

"I love you."

"I love you more." He washed my body as we kissed.

We stepped out of the shower with smiles on our faces. There was nothing wrong with hot sex in the morning. It will help your day go better. Both of you will think about it all day and smile. It's healing for your relationship. Trust me. I knew.

I fixed breakfast and as we ate, we smiled and giggled like high school kids.

"Baby, I got to go to work," Keith let me know as if I didn't.

I walked him to the door. We kissed for a second, and he grabbed my ass.

"Stop. You know you can't finish."

"I can stay if you want me to. I'm the boss."

"Go to work. I got to clean up and then go check on my own business."

"We'll finish this up tonight."

"I got you."

"Bye." We kissed again.

I watched him leave in his black on black Bentley. I closed the door thinking about our wild night and morning.

I called my mother on my cell while I changed the sheets on the bed.

"Hello," she answered.

"Mom, did you take the kids to school for me?"

"Yeah."

"Thanks, mom. You the best. Need anything?"

"I'm good."

"Okay. I love you."

"Love you too, baby."

I hung up and called my beauty supply store. I had one of my friends running it for me. I was not a stupid bitch. If that nigga decided to leave me, I'd have something to fall back on. You'd never see me like Angela Bassett was in *Waiting to Exhale*. I would not be left with nothing. I got some money from him and opened a beauty supply store where people could buy their supplies.

I'd been thinking about opening a salon with my best friend, Jackie. The bitch could do some hair. I just needed to find a location.

"Hey girl, what's up?" I asked.

"Nothing. It's all good over here."

"Well, I'll be in today to help you."

"Fine wit' me."

"See you in a few."

I finished making the bed and put on a pair of blue Guess jeans with a white and blue Guess shirt. After sliding on a pair of blue stiletto heeled boots, I brushed my hair, grabbed my purse and left.

Robert Baptiste

Chapter 2

Keith

As I pulled up to my company on old Gentily Road, I spotted two Federal Agents sitting in an unmarked gray Ford Taurus with dark tinted windows. They were taking pictures of my company.

See those motherfuckers had been on my ass since I beat their ass in trial. The Feds didn't like it when you won, especially since they had planted the drugs in my car in the first place. Then I went legit on their ass and started a construction company worth over $50 million. Not bad for a nigga straight out of the Calliope Projects, one of the worst areas in New Orleans.

They thought I was using the company as a front for selling drugs. The Feds knew I used to provide the whole city with bricks of cocaine. I was moving over two thousand kilos a month. I was plugged in with a Mexican cartel. The Feds didn't think I could just leave all of that, but I did.

I made a promise to Shantell once we had a daughter that I was done, and I meant it. My word was all I had in this world. Plus, Shantell had been with me through all the bullshit, the lying and the cheating. She never knew how big I was on the streets. She knew I sold drugs. She just never knew how much or all the shit I was into in the streets.

After I moved my last hundred, I paid Deloso his money, and I was out. So, the Feds were trying to bust me on some back in the day bullshit. But there was nothing left to tie me to it. I cut all ties with the nigga I left all my shit to, but the Feds keep trying. They knew what I used to be when I had the city on lock. I had crooked police. Bodies came up missing. Witnesses were found without heads in dumpsters, and niggas were left in cars with bullet holes in their heads. I had an efficient and vicious team that didn't mind putting in work.

The Feds never caught me doing anything. I was a step ahead of them on everything. I knew when the heat would come down. They'd never caught me slipping.

I walked over to their car and tapped on the window. The window rolled down and a white Tommy Lee Jones and a black Will Smith looking agent looked up at me. They both wore black suits.

"I see it's the Men in Black," I said. "Can I help you?

"We need you to come down to the station and talk."

"You don't need me to do shit. Also, this is private property. So, move along before I call my lawyer on ya' punk asses."

"All of this can go away if you will just answer a few questions."

"I'm not going nowhere. Ya'll motherfuckers need to leave right now."

"We're going, but we'll be back."

I watched as they pulled off. I stalked into my office and slammed my briefcase on my desk. "Get Baldwin on the phone."

"Yes, sir. "

Damn, I thought he took care of this shit with these motherfuckers. I can believe these motherfuckers are still harassing me. It doesn't look good for me business if the Feds keep coming around my company

"Baldwin's on line one."

"Thanks." I angrily punched line one. "Man, I thought you took care of this Feds shit."

"I did."

"So why these motherfuckers still on my line and coming to my company to take pictures."

"What did they want?"

"They asked me to come to the federal building and answer a few questions."

"Same old shit, then. Okay, I'll handle it. Don't worry. I'm sure it's nothing

"Man, please get on top of it. It don't look good for my business."

"Relax. I'm on it."

I slammed the phone down and sat in my chair. I took a deep breath, slowly releasing the air. I started thinking. I hoped Dave hadn't managed to get me involved in some new shit. Dave was my righthand man on the streets. I turned everything over to him when I got out of the game. *I hope this nigger ain't got busted and running his mouth to the Feds.*

I started to pick up the phone and call him, but I stopped. If the Feds had his phone tapped and heard me talking to him, I was going to be fucked. They wanted to tie me to a conspiracy. Damn, I hoped a nigga's past didn't come back to bite me in the ass.

"Boss, your wife's on line two."

I picked up.

"Hey, baby," she said.

"Baby girl! What's up?"

"I wanted to tell you I love you. I can't wait to see you tonight."

"I love you too."

"What's wrong? I hear something in your voice. It doesn't sound right."

"It's nothing. I just got a lot of work stuff on my plate."

"Baby, don't let it stress you out. I got you when you get off."

"I'm not, but I am looking forward to us tonight."

As I hung up, my secretary called out, "Baldwin's on line three."

"What did you find out?"

"I looked into it. They're investigating an alleged former associate. They wanted to try to get you to help them."

"Hell, no. I'm not trying to help them motherfuckers with nothing."

"Fine."

"Look, find out who this person is?"

"I will. Look, take your wife on a nice vacation for a couple of weeks. When you get back everything will be settled."

"Sounds like a plan. Talk to you in a couple of weeks." I sat back in the chair. Blowing out hot air, I was thinking a vacation would be nice. I picked up the phone calling me wife.

"Hello."

"Look, find a babysitter and pack our stuff. As a matter of fact, don't pack shit. We'll buy there. We going on a vacation to one of your favorite spots.

"Miami?

"That's right.'

"Bye, I'm on the phone with a sitter now."

I told my secretary before I left the office, "I'm going on vacation. If something important comes up hit me on the phone."

"Will do, sir."

Chapter 3

Dave

I was in one of my trap houses counting money. I knew the Feds were on me, so I was getting as much cash as I could together. A nigga might've needed to shoot down to Mexico. I knew if I made it there, there wouldn't be any more corning back, and those motherfuckers couldn't touch me there.

I had sent my bitch, Dana, out to put the bags in the car, but I was thinking why was it taking this hoe so long to come back for the stuff?

I grabbed the money and crammed it in the bag. As I went for the door it exploded inward and federal agents rushed in pointing guns at me. "Get on the floor, now motherfucker!"

Ain't this a bitch?

I dropped the money and lay on the floor. Agents put their knees painfully in my back as they handcuffed me. They lifted me up and patted me down for weapons before reading me my rights. Then I was marched outside where I saw my girl in the back of a car.

They took us to the FBI headquarters where they put us in separate interrogation rooms. I didn't worry about her. She didn't know shit. I was just fucking her. She was one of many side pieces I had in the city.

Two FBI agents came in carrying folders. One was a fine dark-skinned chick wearing a gray suit and black heels. The other was a tall, bald, black man. He was in a black suit. They reminded me of Regina King and Morris Chestnut. They sat at the table, facing me. "Okay, Dave. It's time for you to help yourself."

"What you mean, help myself?"

"Well, I've seized five hundred kilograms of cocaine. Most of your people are singing like birds. You're looking at a life sentence." the female agent said, "On top of that you're facing conspiracy in a murder for hire on a drug dealer known as Barn. He's on life support. If he dies, it is murder one and the shooter has named you as the one who made the order to kill. That carries a life sentence."

"What's your offer?"

"You give us dirt on Keith Washington. Testify to the murders that you did on his order, and we will give you no more than eleven years. If not, life. Ball' s in your court. Think about it."

They walked out. I grabbed a pack of cigarettes and shake them nervously. I looked at the black tinted one-way window knowing they were staring back at me.

"Fuck a bitch ass nigger ratting on me. Fuck that. I ain't doing life for nobody. Fuck that nigger, Keith. He living the high life. The rules of the game have changed since Keith's day. In this era, it's called get down first." I'm not going to spend the rest of my life in a federal prison while a nigga out here enjoys his life." I blew smoke from my nose.

The agents re-entered the room. "So, what's it going be?" she asked.

"I'll give you the stuff on Keith, but I need this shit in writing and my lawyer present."

"It's done. By the way, we let your friend go as well," the male agent said.

I knew I was doing some down bad shit. All my life Keith looked out for me. That nigga had put me on when I didn't have anybody. When I got out of state prison, I was sleeping in my car. Without a pot to piss in or a window to throw it out of, he took me in his house. I was his kid's godfather, but I couldn't do life for nobody. I was sorry.

He was going to have to respect the game. He'd do the same thing. Those bitches weren't playing fair.

Chapter 4

Shantell

We landed in Miami Friday night. We took a rental car to the Fountainbleu Hotel where Keith had gotten the presidential suite. It was ten thousand dollars a night. When we walked in, I couldn't believe my eyes. It was big and laid out. They provided a butler and maids. A huge marble jacuzzi dominated the bathroom. The bed seemed large enough to hold ten or twelve people. I saw why this motherfucker was called the presidential suite. It was laid out for the President of the United states.

I walked out to Keith who is on the balcony. We looked over the ocean at the reds, oranges, and pinks of the sunset.

"I love you baby," I said as we hugged and kissed.

"I love you back. You like the room?"

"Love it."

"Nothing but the best for you."

"What did I ever to do to deserve you?"

"You love me."

We went back in the suite.

"Come on, baby, let's go check out the club in the hotel. I heard it be lit," I said.

"Okay."

We walked downstairs to LIV. The club was packed from wall to wall with all kinds of people. There were bad bitches and fine ass niggas everywhere. Several famous rappers including Rick Ross and Drake were here. It was off the chain.

We got a spot in the VIP room. Keith ordered bottles of Cîroc. We got drunk and partied all night long. I didn't know how we got back to the hotel room. I hazily remembered Keith and I fucking and then we passed out. I woke up the next morning to a knock at the door. It was the butler bringing us breakfast in bed. It was a large breakfast with bacon, sausage, biscuits, eggs, waffles and fruit including fresh mango. It was served with freshly squeezed orange juice.

I took the cart into the bedroom and woke Keith up. "Baby, the food's here," I said as I kissed him.

He got up and we ate breakfast in bed. "You have fun last night?" he asked.

"Yeah, I had a ball."

"Where you want to go today?"

"I want to take a walk on the beach ... and go shopping."

We got in the shower together and washed one another's body. We also got a quickie in.

I put on my pink thong that had my ass hanging out, looking big and my new Vickie bra that had my titties sitting up right. I wrapped a sarong around my waist, and we left the hotel.

We walked along the South Beach strip. There were so many bars and different foreign cars including Ferraris, Lamborghinis, and Bentleys. There were fine ass women in two-piece bikinis. These women were all complexions, Cuban, Dominican, white and black. The prettiest woman I saw was Puerto Rican and built like a sister. The men were hot too. They walked around half-naked showing off their big arm and chest muscles.

We continued down the strip to Bal Harbor shopping mall and went to Neiman's. They carried all the high-end clothes, shoes, and accessories. We shopped and Keith bought me a lot of clothes, shoes, and jewelry. He spent more than twenty grand on himself.

One of Keith's friends gave him some playoff tickets for the game that night. I had never seen a pro basketball game in person, and I loved Lebron James. I wanted to see him up close and personal. I wanted to see sweat dripping off his body. I had cum many nights while playing with myself and thinking about him. I was a little in love with him. He could get the pussy. I would leave Keith high and dry for him.

I put on some tight, red Louis Vuitton jeans with a white Louis Vuitton button-down blouse, some red open toe red bottoms. I also put on all the jewelry Keith had just bought me and my half a million dollar wedding ring.

Keith was wearing an all-white Gucci outfit with white and red loafers. He was also wearing a platinum blue diamond chain, a Rolex watch and his wedding ring.

Caught Up in the Life

In the arena, it was loud as fuck. Everybody there was wearing their white Heat jerseys, swinging white towels in the air as player introductions were made. We were sitting in the front row with Rick Ross, Trick Daddy, and other super- stars. We took pictures with some of them.

The game was game seven of the NBA. finals. The shit was live. Wade and James looked even finer in person. I thought I would pass out when they walked in front of me. Lebron made a bitch want to drink his bathwater.

I took pictures of James slamming on two different guys. The crowd went crazy when the Heat won the championship. James was the MVP. I even took a selfie with him and Wade in it. My panties were soaking wet. I couldn't believe it.

We left the game and hit a strip club called KOD. It was big as shit. It had three stages with big, fine, butt-naked bitches everywhere. They were shaking their asses and sliding down poles on every stage. There were lots of rappers in the VIP with us. The motherfucker was off the chain.

Keith got ten thousand dollars in ones. I walked over to the stage where a thick, big ass butt-naked Puerto Rican and black chick danced. She had short, blue hair. She was cutting up on the stage and had niggas and hoes throwing her money. She winked at me.

Watching her shake her ass in a guy's face, I went back to the VIP where Keith had a couple of hoes giving him lap dances. As I was sipping on strawberry Cîroc, the chick who was on the stage came over.

"Do you want a lap dance?" She smiled.

"Yes," I said, smiling back.

Keith watched as she gave me a couple of lap dances. I gripped her ass as she bounced up and down on me. "Damn, your ass is soft."

"You like that, huh?" she asked as she started bouncing it even higher in my face.

The next thing I knew, we were leaving the club with her. Back at the hotel, Keith watched me and her eat each other out on the bed. Keith walked over stroking his dick. I grabbed it and deep throated it while she sucked his balls.

We took turns riding his dick. I watched as she rode it in a reverse cowgirl position, bouncing her ass in his face. Then I got in the doggy style position, letting Keith hit me in the ass. He slammed his dick in and out of me as I ate this bitch's pussy out. We took turns letting him fuck our asses. As he was about to cum, he pulls out of me and shot all over our faces.

I sucked his dick until I get him back hard. We fucked him all night. The next evening, we soaked in a hot jacuzzi bath just enjoying each other's company.

Later, we took a casual stroll on the beach. The sun was going down, and it was beautiful. I knew we weren't supposed to be fucking on the beach, but it was so beautiful that I had to.

I lay on the sandy beach and took my thong off. I let Keith make love to me. He went down on me, eating my pussy until my legs started shaking. "Fuck, daddy! I'm cuming!" I held his head down on my pussy as I grinded, cuming all in his mouth.

Keith raised up and put his dick inside me. He fucked me slow, taking his time as the sun went down. Now I knew why Maze called it "the golden time of day."

After making love, we talked about trying for another child. Later, back in the room, Keith's phone rang. He answered. It was his secretary.

"Boss, the Feds have been in the office for the last two days. They're asking questions."

"What did you tell them?"

"Nothing."

I walked in the room shocked at the look on Keith's face. "Okay, I'll be back tomorrow," he said as he hung up.

I walked over to him. "Baby, is everything okay?"

"No problems. Just some business. Look, I'm sorry, but we have to cut this trip short. I got to handle something at the company."

"I understand."

Keith walked up to me and hugged and kissed me. "I'm sorry."

"It's no problem. I had fun. I know you going to make it up to me?"

"Okay, I promise. We'll do it again soon."

"I want to go to Jamaica."

Caught Up in the Life

"It's on. I love you." He tongue kissed me.
We fell back on the bed and made love again.

Robert Baptiste

Chapter 5

Keith

I rushed from the house to my company. Sarsh had called and said two FBI agents were waiting in my office. I called Baldwin, but he was in court fighting a murder case. The two agents were there waiting for me. The same two motherfuckers. I slammed my briefcase on my desk.

"What the fuck are ya'll doing in my office? I told you motherfuckers to stay off my property and not to come back without a. warrant."

"How was the vacation with the wife? Did you enjoy the game? Paying ten thousand a night for the presidential suite?"

"You motherfuckers been following me?"

"That's the job."

I picked up the phone. "Sarsh, get Baldwin on the phone."

"Yes, Mr. Washington."

She didn't have time to make the call.

"We're going to take you to the station. We need to ask you some questions about some recently discovered bodies:"

"Man, I'm not going anywhere with y'all."

"This isn't a request."

"What?"

"You're under arrest. Please turn around." The black guy pulled out his handcuffs.

"Why are you arresting me?"

"Conspiracy to distribute drugs and murder."

"What?"

The black agent handcuffed me and read me my rights.

As we leave my office, I said, "Sarsh, keep calling him."

"Yes, sir."

They didn't take me to the federal building on Camp Street. They took me to federal office on the lake front. I didn't even know this motherfucker was here. The building is constructed with darkly tinted windows everywhere, Inside, there are nothing but FBI agents everywhere. They stick me in an interrogation room with an iron table, three chairs, and a one way dark tinted window.

"I'm going to have you two bitches' badges. I want my lawyer," I screamed as they shut the door and left.

In a few minutes, two other agents walked in. One was a black man and the other was a black woman. He was carrying a folder. After they sat down, she said, "I'm Agent Williams, and this is Agent Wilson."

"Man, I don't give a fuck who y'all are. I want my lawyer."

"That's your right, Mr. Washington, but we got you down here to give you a chance to help yourself."

Help myself. You motherfuckers are trippin' I don't need any help."

The male agent puts the folder down in front of me.

"What the fuck is this?" I ask.

"Dave Green. He's your associate. He was your right-hand man in the murder blood gang you ran."

"I don't know what the fuck y'all talking about. I don't even know this nigga. Where my fucking lawyer at?"

"You claim not to know him? How about this picture of you and him hugging inside a club?"

"So, what that mean? I take pictures in the club with people I don't know all the time."

"Mr. Washington, we want to help you avoid going to Federal Prison for…"

"Help me ." I laugh.

"Your name is continually mentioned in murders all over the city."

I heard a knock on the window. Baldwin walked into the room. "Get your stuff. We're out."

"This is your time to help yourself, Mr. Washington," the female agent said.

"Fuck you and your case," I said as I left.

"Next time you have questions for my client call me first, or I will have your badges," Baldwin added.

I got in Baldwin's car and we drove off.

"Man! I thought you took care of this Fed shit," I said.

"I've spoken with them."

"Well, it wasn't good enough because these motherfuckers are still fucking with me and coming around my company."

"That's not good for my business."

"I understand, but this is complicated."

"They asked me questions about that Dave shit."

"I'll ask around and find out what's going on."

"Keep me posted."

Baldwin had been my lawyer since the streets. He helped me and my crew beat lots of drugs and murder cases. The Feds were on him at one time because of the way he was winning cases, but they never found anything. He was clean. They mainly wanted to fuck with him because he represented me. After I left the streets, I made him my corporate lawyer and paid him two hundred stacks a month.

I knew he was the best in the city when he got all my guys off who had been busted with two hundred keys of coke. Since then, he's been a part of the team.

"Man, I'll call you later," I said as I got out of his car.

"Later."

I got in my car to drive home. Damn, shit is looking fucked up for me right now. I need to get word out on the streets and have this nigga killed. I still had a little juice on the streets, but if they missed, and the Feds on this nigga's line, I was really fucked then.

As I got closer to him, I yelled, "Fuck!" and hit the steering wheel. I walked in to find Shantel cooking dinner. I hugged and kissed her.

"Hey, baby! you home early. Is everything all right?"

I wanted to tell her. I really did, but I didn't want to stress her right now with things going so good between us.

"Everything's fine. Where the kids at?"

"My mother's going to drop them off in a little while."

"Okay, I love you."

"I love you too." She tongue kissed me.

We got in a quickie there in the kitchen right before the kids came home.

Robert Baptiste

Chapter 6

Keith

The next day I was sitting in my office doing paperwork when my phone rang. "Hello," I answered.

"Man, your boy Dave got busted about a week ago by the Feds. He's being held in an undisclosed location," Baldwin said.

"What do they have on him?"

"Conspiracy to sell five hundred kilos of cocaine."

"Dumb motherfucker."

"That's not even the worst. They got him on murder for hire. He paid some guy to kill an undercover agent, but he didn't kill him. The guy got busted and told on Dave to the Feds."

"So, what the nigga looking at?"

"Life."

"Damn, this shit ain't looking good. I need you tell him something."

"Man, you heard what I said. The Feds got this nigga. It would not be a good look for you to be fucking with this nigga right now."

"So, what I'm supposed to do?"

"Hope this nigga stay solid."

"Thanks, man. Keep me posted on anything else you hear."

"Will do."

Keith hung up.

Damn, I thought. I needed to tell my wife about this shit, but I needed to see if he going to stay sold.

"Your wife's on line one."

"Thanks, put her through."

"Okay."

"Hello, baby," I greeted her.

"I wanted to know if you could come home early tonight."

"Yeah, I can. Why?'

"Because I'm thinking me, you and somebody else might have a little fun tonight. The kids are at my mother's house."

"Sure, hook it up, baby."

"I love you."

"Love you back."

I did want to tell her, but she'd think I was back in the game. Or she'd think I never got out and had been lying to her all this time. She might've thought the construction company was just a cover up to sell drugs. I did not have time for the bullshit. I had enough shit on my plate without having to worry about my wife's bullshit.

I jumped in my car and looked in the review mirror. The Feds were there. They'd been following me for a couple of days now. They were taking pictures. Baldwin said I had to let them do this shit as long as they respected my rights. It was just a part of an ongoing investigation.

Baldwin wanted me to play it cool, so they could see I was not part of the game. I needed to show that I was not affiliated with Dave and his gang. Shit, my whole life could be destroyed.

"Fuck!" I shouted to myself.

I thought once I got out of the game, this shit wouldn't come back on me, but I was wrong. Man, was I wrong. If I'd known this shit, I would've just stayed in the game.

I had the best plug in the South. I was dealing with the Gulf Coast Cartel. There never was a drought with them. I was getting two to five thousand kilos a month. Paying eight grand a key, I sold them for 12.5 All I really had to do was make sure my people got it and collected the money. I was tied at the hip with the head cartel boss, Deloso He basically ran everything in the southern US, Louisiana, Mississippi, Alabama, Georgia, Florida and Texas.

None of that was important now, especially if this nigga didn't stay solid. If he got to talking, he knew where the bodies were buried. He was one of my righthand men. If he was talking, it would sink me.

* * *

SHANTELL

I got home at about four o'clock and started cooking dinner. I had left the kids with my mother and hit Icy up, but she had other plans. I couldn't find another bitch at the last minute.

So, it was going to be Keith and me, which I didn't mind. I always had tricks up my sleeves. I was a freaky bitch. Icy just added a little extra spice in the bedroom. You had to keep things fresh in there. A bitch got tired of the same shit. Most of the time that was is why men and women cheat. Just dropping a few jewels on y'all.

As I was about to go upstairs to take my bath, I heard the doorbell. I was not expecting anyone. Keith had his own keys. Besides, the guard at the gate never called.

I looked through the peephole. There were two men in black suits. They looked like Feds. I started feeling butterflies in my stomach. The Feds only came to your house for two reasons and that was taxes or to put somebody's ass in jail.

I took a deep breath and opened the door. I tried to hide my nervousness. I wondered why they were here. I looked them over. One was an older black man who reminded me of Morgan Freeman. The other was a younger Brad Pitt look alike.

"Can I help y'all," I asked.

"I'm Special Agent Price, and this is Special Agent Smith," the older man said as he showed me his badge. "Do you mind if we come in to ask you a few questions."

"Yes, I mind."

"Well, is your husband home?"

"No, he's not. What is this about?"

"We have a few questions for him as well."

"About what?"

"Mrs. Washington. We can't talk about that out here. Are you sure we can't come in?"

"I'm sure."

See Keith told me if these motherfuckers ever came to the house, don't let them in. All they wanted to do is look around to see how you're living. They wanted to know how you could afford your stuff, which was none of their fucking business. They were trying to build a case.

"Let you husband know we came by. Tell him that we need to talk. If you ever want to talk, call me. Here's my card."

I took the card and shut the door in their faces. I leaned against the door. It felt like my heart was trying to bust out of my chest. It was beating so hard. I stumbled to the sofa. I tried to collect my thoughts and figure out why the Feds were looking for Keith. The only thing that came to my mind was that he'd gone back to selling drugs or had never quit. His company was a front to keep the Feds and me off his back. I wanted to ask him, but he lied to me before when he said he had stopped selling drugs.

The last time I believed him. I thought he'd quit. How could he do this to us? He had a million dollar company, two great kids, and a bad freak wife willing to do anything for him. Why would he be so stupid to jeopardize our family like that?

Tears started rolling down my face. "Fuck." I screamed as I pushed all the books off the coffee table.

The phone rang. I looked and saw it was Keith. I snatched the phone up mad as hell.

"Hey, baby," he said.

"Motherfucker, don't baby me."

"Hold up, Shantell. Bring you voice down and tell what's going on?"

"Like you don't know. You tell me what's going on?"

"Baby, stop tripping. Let me know what's going on."

"Don't play dumb with me right now."

"Man, tell me what the fuck you talking about?"

"The fucking Feds showed up at the house today. They were looking for your ass."

"Is that what got you so bent out of shape? It's probably nothing. I think I owe some tax shit. I'll get the lawyer on it right now."

"Oh, I thought you was back on the street selling drugs."

"What? Why would you think that?"

"I don't know what to think."

"Now I'm mad. I'll see you later."

"Keith, don't be like that."

"Bye, Shantell." He hung up the phone in my face.

I sat back on the couch with my head in my hands. I was crying and thinking. Should I believe that this was about some tax shit? I knew it was fucked up, but Keith lied to me about this street shit before. I loved Keith to death, but when it came to the streets it seemed that he can't let them go. I got dressed and drove to Keshon's house. I got out of the car with tears streaming down my face.

I knocked on the door.

"Who is it?" she asked.

"Me."

She opened the door and looked at me." What's wrong?"

"Can I come in?"

"Sure." She hugged me.

I sat on her couch. Tears were still running down my face. "I think Keith's back to selling drugs."

"What? Are you sure?"

"Yes. No... I'm not sure."

"So, what makes you say that?"

"The Feds showed up at our house looking for him."

"What? Did they say for what?

"No. Look, I need something strong to drink. And bring me some of that weed you smoking on. A bitch's head is hurting."

"I got you."

She left and quickly returned with a blunt and some Patron. "Here."

"Thanks."

I swallowed the whole glass, feeling it burning my insides. Then I hit the weed and started choking.

"Damn! This some good fucking weed."

"Yeah, it's dro."

"This shit is good," I said, hitting it again. I passed it to her. "I need to get some of this shit."

"I didn't know you smoke."

"I didn't, but after the Feds showed up at my house, I do now."

I refilled my glass with Patron but sipped it this time. "What do you think I need to do?"

"Talk to him and see what's really going on. A man likes for you to talk to him, not at him. Don't go all crazy and shit because for real, you won't get the answers you're looking for. Go home and fuck and suck him real good. Then when you're both relaxed, you can talk to him. He'll tell you everything you want to know."

"I hear you. Look, girl, I got to go. I had a night planed for us, but that's all fucked up. I might as well go get my kids. Thanks for the talk. I needed it."

"Are you sure you can drive."

"I'm buzzed, but I'm good. By the way, I'm taking this blunt home with me."

"It's all good, and everything is going to work out for you and Keith. You'll see," she said hugging me.

"Shit, you give good advice. Why can't you use it in your own relationships?"

"Good question."

When I go in the house with the kids, Keith is on the phone. The kids run up to him trying to talk.

"Daddy, Daddy," they said.

"Hey, y'all give daddy a second. I'm on the phone."

"Okay." They ran to their rooms.

"Y'all get ready for dinner," I yelled as they ran.

"Okay, mom."

I sat on the couch watching him. I was high as a motherfucker. I went to the kitchen to get a bag of chips and returned to watch Keith on the phone.

Whatever was being said wasn't good. The expression on his face said it all.

He hung up and sat next to me on the couch. He closed his eyes and appears to be in deep thought.

"So, who was that on the phone?"

"The lawyer."

"What was he talking about?"

"I need to go in to see what they're talking about. He's setting up an appointment in the morning."

I turned around to face him and looked deep in his eyes. "Keith, I love you. If you went back to the street life, let me know. Don't keep me in the dark. I've been with you through thick and thin. We're married. That means we're partners. You can tell me anything."

"All this time we've been together, and you still don't trust me or believe in me, huh? I was thinking all this time you had my back. The one motherfucking person I thought I could depend on. I see you just like everybody else."

He went to the bedroom, slamming the door behind him. A few minutes later, I got up to follow him. He was lying on the bed watching Sports Center.

"Keith ..." I entered the bedroom.

"Don't start no shit, Shantell. I'm not in the mood for it. I got a lot of shit on my mind."

I slid into the bed and put my head on his chest. As I listened to his heartbeat, he played with my hair. I knew he really wasn't mad. If he was, he wouldn't let me touch him.

"Keith, I'm sorry for not believing you. I love you. Whatever you're going through, I'll be there for you. I got your back one hundred percent. I don't doubt that. I promise you I'm here for the long haul." I kissed him as I got up.

"So, you still think I'm lying to you, huh? I never had to lie to you since we got married. Okay, I lied a few times when I was in the thug life in the streets. But it was only because I didn't want you to get caught up in none of that shit if the Feds came. You and the kids would be safe. That was ten years ago. So, I'll answer your question. No, I'm not selling drugs, and I haven't lied about nothing in the ten years we've been married."

"So, you won't mind if I go to the Federal building with you tomorrow?"

"That's fine with me."

I went back to the kitchen to get supper on the table. What was I going to do if this motherfucker went to prison? I'd have to raise these kids myself. Worse, I would have to hear from my mother how she told me the motherfucker was no good.

My daughter walked in as tears streamed down my face. "Mama, why you crying?"

"Baby girl, I'm not crying. I just finished cutting up onions."

"They make you cry?"

"Yes, baby, they do." I smiled. Her big, brown eyes made her look like her father. "Go wash your hands and tell your brother it's time to eat."

I set the table, and we sat down to dinner. They started talking to their dad.

"You owe me ten dollars for getting good grades in school," Keith Jr. said.

"And me too, daddy," Kawine spoke up.

"Hold up. Y'all gonna have to show me these grades."

"All right." They ran to their rooms and brought back their report cards.

"See," Keith Jr. said.

"Now, give us our money," Kawine added.

They smiled holding out their hands.

"Here y'all go," he said as he handed them money.

"Thank you."

"Y'all get ready for bed."

"Love you, Daddy," they both said as they hugged him goodnight.

I stayed up half the night, tossing and turning. It was stressful to think about how quick life could turn around in one day. We were going to see the Feds, and there was no guarantee his black ass would be coming back. I knew this shit was bigger than taxes. I didn't care what Keith said. It had something to do with his past life. I just had a gut feeling.

I got out of bed and went to the bathroom. I lit the blunt, getting high to try to ease the stress away.

Chapter 7

Shantell

We pull up to the federal building on Camp Street the next morning. Baldwin pulled in behind us in his black 550 S.L. Benz. All the times I passed this big, white building with the big, white steps in front of it, I never knew it was a federal court building. I used to see people going in and out of it dressed in suits, but I never thought they were federal agents. I guess I thought it was a law firm. I never thought in a million years I'd be going to a federal building.

Keith got out of his black Range Rover. He was wearing a gray suit with matching gator shoes. He opened my door and helped me out. I was wearing a red Fendi dress with red and white Fendi open toe heels.

Baldwin got out of his car and straightened his black pin stripe suit. Baldwin was short, black and bald. He looked like the lead singer of Silk. He walked over to us, shook Keith's hand and spoke to me, "Hey, Shantell."

"Baldwin."

"Keith, when we go in, let me handle the talking. You just listen."

"Okay."

As we entered, we were greeted by two, big, white agents who looked like wrestlers. They took us down the hallway to a room that had two, gray chairs outside it.

"Baby, you can stay out here," Keith said.

"No, I want to come in with you," I said as I held his hand tight.

"Come on in."

The empty room had cheap, dark blue carpet on the floor. A large wooden table dominated the room. It was surrounded by black leather chairs.

"Have a seat. The prosecutor will be here in a moment," the agent said.

"Remember, I do the talking," Baldwin repeated to Keith.

I was nervous as shit. It probably looked like I was the one waiting to be questioned. I looked over to see that Keith was whispering something in Baldwin's ear. He didn't seem nervous at all. It was kind of fucking me up. If I was selling drugs and the Feds wanted to talk to me, I would be scared shitless, but Keith had been down this road before. He had beat them on a gun charge. I guess he knew what he was up against. But I was fucked up in this bitch because I was the only one in the room that didn't know what was going on. Keith was being especially secretive about shit, especially about the streets. I knew this was about more than taxes when those motherfuckers showed up at the house looking for his ass.

My thoughts were interrupted by a slim, tall, white guy with glasses. He was wearing cheap black slacks, a white button-down shirt, and some cheap looking black loafers. He walked to the table and laid down two folders.

"How everybody? I'm Michael Vance. I'm the U.S. attorney for this district. I will be handling this case. Let's get to the point. We're seeking an indictment against Mr. Washington."

I'm sure you are, I thought.

"We have been seeking to bring charges against Mr. Washington for more than ten years. His business is legitimate now, but at one time he distributed large volumes of cocaine throughout New Orleans. We also believe that he was responsible for several murders, though we never had sufficient evidence to get a conviction."

"This seems to be speculative. You can't possibly know my client partook in these actions," Baldwin interjected.

"But we do. We have a lot of witnesses willing to testify that your client ordered hits on various drug dealers. We also have evidence that he was moving five thousand kilograms of cocaine per month. Look at these." He slid some pictures in front of Baldwin and Keith. "You can see headless bodies. Many were killed by gunfire. All are hits either ordered or performed by Mr. Washington."

Looking at the pictures, I was sickened and shocked. I knew Keith had been a drug dealer, but I didn't know he'd killed people. I looked at him with a fucked up look on my face. I wanted to say something, but I kept my mouth closed.

"What are you offering?" Baldwin asked.

"We want Deloso. Your client serves him up, he goes free."

"I'm not giving you shit." Keith looked the prosecutor dead in the eyes.

I saw that Keith was fucked up just because the prosecutor asked him about this Deloso person. I didn't know who he was. I had never seen him or even heard Keith talk about him.

"Hold on, Keith. Let me handle this. You claim you have witnesses?"

"We do.... on your client. But we want Deloso, and we don't have anyone as close to the Gulf Coast Cartel as Mr. Washington. He was one of Deloso's righthand men. When Keith got out of dealing, he plugged his righthand man Dave Green in with the cartel, but Deloso lets Mr. Green deal with his mules. Isn't that right, Mr. Washington?"

"Man, I don't have to tell your bitch ass nothing. You can get the fuck out my face and get it out your fucking head if you think I'm going to rat. Fuck you and them witnesses."

He stood up.

"Hold on a minute, Keith." Baldwin stood as well.

"Shantell, get you shit. We out this bitch."

I grabbed my purse and followed Keith out of the room. Baldwin ran up behind us. "Keith, think about this."

"Baldwin, I ain't trying to hear the shit this motherfucker is talking about. He's trying to make me out to be a rat. Fuck that motherfucker."

"Keith, if you don't take the deal, you will face thirty to life."

"Well put on your best trial suit. We're going to put twelve in the box."

"Okay, I will see what I can do. Let me go see what else they're talking about."

"Yeah, you do that."

It was a long ride home. I had butterflies in my stomach the whole way. We didn't even say two words to one another. We sat there in complete silence. I was still in shock from all I heard about my husband. My fucking head was still spinning. I needed to hit a blunt and get fucking drunk for real.

I thought I knew my husband. To find out all this shit was more than I could handle.

We pulled up to the house. Keith went in without saying a word. I sat in the car for a minute, still trying to take everything in. I walked in the house, went straight to the bar, grabbed a glass, filled it with Jack Daniels, and gulped it down. I went to the bathroom, lit the blunt, and hit it. I choked on it, getting high as a motherfucker. I walked in the room high as a kite and got in bed next to Keith.

"Baby, we need to talk."

"About what?"

What happened today."

"What do you want to know?"

I sat down Indian style. "Was all that stuff true? What that man said about you."

"Yeah. How do you think we've been living good for all these years?"

"Why didn't you feel you could tell me the truth about those things?"

"It is not about me not trusting you. I told you this day might come, and I didn't want you in the middle of this shit. Because they would threaten you and try to take the kids to get at me. I don't need that stress on my back."

I exhaled as I took it all in. As I looked Keith in his face, I realized I loved him and would be there for him no matter the outcome. "Baby, I love you, and I'm going to be there for you no matter what. We in this shit together," I said climbing on his lap to tongue kiss him.

"Your ass been drinking, and you look high as fuck."

"I needed something strong after all the shit I heard today."

"It's all good. We'll make it through this. I promise."

"Baby, why didn't you tell on this Deloso guy and get this over with?"

"I can't. The line of business I was in and the type of people I dealt with meant you would get killed doing shit like that."

I stripped and climbed on top of him. riding his dick while looking deep into his eyes. I hoped he knew what he was doing.

I got up in the middle of the night because I couldn't sleep. I looked at my sound asleep husband and went to the living room to pour myself a drink. I sat on the couch just crying and thinking. How was I going to make it if this nigga went to prison? Those motherfuckers said he was facing thirty to life. Our kids would be old, and my pussy would have gray hair on it when he got out. How the fuck was I supposed to move on? No man out here wanted a bitch with two kids. It was going to crush me and the kids if he went to prison. What the fuck had I gotten myself into? I was living here with a cold-blooded murderer and one of the city's biggest drug dealers.

I fell asleep on the couch and was awakened by Keith talking to someone on the phone. I grabbed two cups of coffee from the kitchen. As I took one to Keith, he was sitting on the couch in deep thought.

"Here you go. Who was that on the phone?"

"Fuck!" Keith threw the cup against the wall.

I wasn't going to lie. It scared the hell out of me. I never saw him this upset before. "Baby, what's going on? Talk to me?"

He paced back and forth, rubbing his hand on his head as he took several deep breaths. "That was Baldwin." He looked at me, "That motherfucker Dave is the one testifying against me."

"What? Your best friend Dave?"

"Yeah, that motherfucker got caught and cut a deal with the Feds."

"Shit, so what does that mean?"

"I'm fucking hit. He was my right hand. I left that bitch ass nigga everything He was one of the motherfuckers that did a lot of killing for me."

"Can you get to him?"

"The nigga's in the witness protection program. The Feds got him protected."

"Shit, Shit! So, baby, you need to tell on this Deloso person. Tell them everything you know about him."

"Hell fuck no. That's not an option. I'm not a rat."

"So, what the fuck me and the kids supposed to do when your ass go to prison for thirty years? Tell me that?"

"Y'all going to be straight with money if that's what you worrying about."

I got in his face. "Nigga, you think all I'm worried about is some fucking money? Fuck that! What about the kids? What about me? I need you."

"Man, get the fuck out my face. This shit is bigger than all that."

"What the fuck you talking about? What can be bigger than you family, huh? Nigga, you tripping for real now."

"I don't want to talk about this shit no more," he walked off.

"Fuck!" I slammed the door behind me as I walked out. I got in my car and drove around the city. I was looking for answers to answer my husband's question.

What could be bigger than your family? Nothing came to my mind. I was really fucked up in the head. My life was really fucking over.

Chapter 8

Shantell

Keith and I were in the bed butt-naked after some hot make-up sex that we had been having for the last couple of months following our big argument. I was still trying to understand this code of the street shit Keith had with this guy. Despite all the hot, sweaty make-up sex, Keith still didn't give me the answer I was looking for on this family thing.

So, I let it go for a while. I was glad I was getting some because the nigga had put me on ban for a week. I needed some dick to relieve stress. The weed helped some, but the dick was better.

We had gone to court a couple of times, but he and the prosecutor was still beefing.

As I was about to get up, the front door crashed open. I was trying to grab some clothes when I realized a lot of men had guns drawn on us.

"Don't fucking move," the blonde FBI agent yelled, pointing his gun at me and Keith.

"Don't talk to my wife like that," Keith said.

"Shut the fuck up and get on the floor."

"Fuck you, pig. I ain't doing shit."

They rushed Keith, wrestled him to the floor and put handcuffs on him. They let me get up and put on my robe.

"Y'all got a warrant," I asked with my arms folded.

"Here you go. Read it."

I grabbed the paper. "Fuck," I said mostly to myself.

I watched as they read Keith his rights. They escorted him from the house to the back of an FBI car. Keith didn't say shit. He just smiled and winked at me to let me know that everything would be all right. He had told me ahead of time that they were coming to get him.

After they pulled off, I went inside to call Baldwin.

Baldwin answered, "Hello."

"It's Shantell. They came and got him a few minutes ago."

"Everything's going to be all right. I'm on top of it."

"Okay."

I hung up. I was glad the kids weren't here to see that shit. They stayed at a friend's house.

I walked over to the bar, grab the bottle of Jack and hit it straight out the bottle. I went to the bathroom and hit the blunt, choking, getting high as fuck. I heard the phone and saw it was from an unknown number. I knew it had to be Keith.

"Hello," I said.

A disembodied voice greeted me. "You have a collect call from Keith Washington. Press one to accept the call…"

I quickly hit one.

"Hey baby, I called the lawyer. He's on the way there. Are you all right?"

"Thanks, and I'm good."

"I love you. Do you need me to do something else?"

"No, I'm good. I'll be home in a minute."

"I know. I'm just glad the kids weren't here to see that shit."

"Me too."

"Love you."

"Love you back."

***

I sat in the cold courtroom nervous as hell waiting for Keith to walk through the door. I watched Baldwin getting ready as he waited for the Marshals to bring Keith in.

Finally, they brought Keith and a few more people in. Keith still had on the clothes he was wearing when they arrested him. He needed a haircut. Baldwin had told me to bring some clothes because the judge would probably grant bond. He did warn me that it could be denied because Keith's charges normally didn't lead to bail. So, I had my fingers, toes, ass and everything else you can cross crossed. I was praying to God that Keith could come home.

It had only been twenty four hours, but I missed him already. Keith looked at me and mouthed that he loved me. I told him the same back. I saw the fat, black judge waddle into the court. He was wearing a black robe and some big glasses. His hair was completely gray. "You may be seated," he instructed.

54

He read his docket and looked up at Keith. "Mr. Washington, do you understand what you're being charged with?" the judge asked.

"Yes, your honor."

"For the record. You are charged with conspiracy to commit capital murder and conspiracy to sell more than two thousand kilograms of cocaine. How do you plead?"

"Not guilty, your honor."

"I see that you own a construction company and have been a solid citizen for the last ten years. I've been going around granting you bond. I'm in a good mood, and I'm not happy with the government's actions in this case. Thus, I will grant bond."

"But your honor," the prosecutor said.

"You can appeal it if you wish, but I'm granting Mr. Washington bond at one million dollars."

"Thank you, your honor," Keith said.

I grabbed my purse and left the court room. His bond was already posted, and Keith left the court room with Baldwin. I ran over to them and started hugging and kissing Keith. I took his hand and led him to the truck to drive home.

At home, I walked in the bathroom, pulled the curtain back and smiled when I saw his hard dick. I stepped in front of him, dropped to my knees and began to deep throat his dick like I never had before. I sucked on his balls and everything.

I stood and he went down on me, eating my pussy out. I turned around and he bent me over. He was eating my asshole like groceries and eating my pussy from the back letting me cum all in his face.

He took me to the bed and began to beat up my pussy like a wild man. He flipped me over hitting me from the back, slamming his dick in and out of me as he fingerfucked my ass. He made me cum back to back as he hit my G-spot.

I knew I was going to get pregnant from the way this nigga was fucking me and how I was throwing this ass back on him. I got on top and rode his dick as he grabbed my ass, bouncing me up and down on his dick. We began to shake together. I bounced harder and felt him shoot all his hot cum in me as I released mine all over his dick. I leaned forward on his chest, still cuming while tongue kissing him. I lay on top of him for a few minutes with my pussy thumping on his dick. We lay in our bed covered with sweat and bodily fluids, telling each other how much we loved one another.

***

For the next couple of weeks, we fucked like dogs. Icy was over a couple of times. I was fucking him like he was the last man on earth since I didn't know when they might come and take him to jail. We had even taken the kids to Disney World for a vacation.

Soon, Keith was called back to court for another bond hearing. In the courtroom, I prayed to God to let him stay out until his trial. The government appealed the bond decision because they weren't happy that Keith wasn't cooperating in the effort to bust this drug lord.

Baldwin entered the courtroom and whispered something to Keith as the judge came into the courtroom.

"You may be seated," he read his docket and adjusted his glasses. "Mr. Washington, the prosecutor's office was successful in its appeal of my decision to grant bond. The appeals court cited your role as leader of a ruthless gang responsible for numerous murders, and they feel that you are a leader in the street gang known as the Murders Calliope gang. Thus, I must revoke your bond. "

"But, you honor," Baldwin began.

"Not now, Mr. Baldwin. Marshals, please take Mr. Washington into custody.

My heart dropped to my ass as I tried to hold back my tears. Keith looked at me and said," I love you."

"Love you back."

I watched as they handcuffed him and walk him out of the courtroom. I fast walked to my car and pulled away crying.

At home, I went straight to the bedroom, grabbed one of his T-shirts that still smelled like him, fell in the bed and balled up crying.

Two weeks passed, and I talked to him on the phone a few times. I was still waiting for him to get me approved on his visitation list. The kids kept asking where their father was. I told them he was working out of town. I didn't want them to know he was in jail yet. I knew it was a fucked up thing to do, but I felt they were too young for this right now.

I tried to go to work and not think about all this mess, but it was impossible. I didn't know how I could go on without him. I walked in my store and saw Ke'shon making a sale. I went to my office trying unsuccessfully not to think about Keith. I felt myself tearing up and started to cry. I tried to stop when I heard the door open, but I couldn't. I was hurting on the inside for real. I was missing my husband so bad.

Ke'shon came over and hugged me. She knew what I was going through. She had caught me crying in my office several times. She was a real friend. She stayed by my side the whole way. She even watched my kids sometimes when I needed some space to clear my head.

"It's going to be all right," she said rubbing my back.

"Not this time. They indicted him on murder and selling drugs. He's looking at thirty to life."

"What the fuck?"

"Ke'shon, I don't know what I'm going to do if he gets thirty years. I'm going to have to raise two kids by myself."

"I'll be there to help you."

"Thanks. I love you."

"I love you back."

My phone rang. I looked at it and saw it was Keith. I wiped my face. "I got to take this. It's Keith."

"All right." She left.

We went through the collect call bit. "Hey, baby," I said, trying to sound upbeat. I didn't want him to know I had been crying and cracking up.

"Hey, love of my life. I was calling to tell you that you can come see me now. Visitation is Saturday and Sunday at eight in the morning and twelve in the afternoon."

"I'll be there."

"All right. Are you okay? Your voice sound funny."

"It's okay. I'm just getting over a cold." I lied because I couldn't tell him the truth.

"My time is about up. Tell the kids I love them. I love you too."

"Love you more."

57

I cried some more as I hung up, but a light went off in my head. I said aloud to the empty office, "Bitch, you need to pull yourself together. You a boss bitch."

I wiped my eyes and fixed my clothes. I could get through this. This was just a minor setback for a major comeback. I needed to convince Keith that he needed to give this Deloso guy up. Maybe jail had changed his mind.

I sure hoped so. I needed my man home. I missed him so much.

Chapter 9

Shantell

I got up the next morning, jumped in the shower, and took a long one. I let the hot water run over my body. It felt so good I didn't want to get out. I was so happy that I was going to see Keith today. I had left the kids at my mother's house last night.

I'd been having to hear that I told you shit for the last couple of weeks. I tried to explain that Keith wasn't back in the streets. It was just that his past had come back to bite him in the ass. But she wasn't trying to hear it. So now, I just drop the kids off and keep moving. I didn't have time for the bullshit. I have a lot of shit on my plate that I was dealing with.

The one thing I made her ass promise me was that she wouldn't tell my kids about their father being in jail. I told her if she did, she wasn't going to see them anymore. I knew it was a messed up thing to do, but I had to threaten her ass because she got a big fucking mouth. She would put my business in the streets for the world to know.

I got out of the shower and put on some peach Victoria's Secret lotion. I put on my red thong and bra. It was summer in New Orleans, and humidity is always as high as fuck. Having second thoughts, I took off the thong and bra, going commando. My pussy needed to breath anyway. She'd been on fire the last couple of weeks anyway. I hadn't played with her for a while or got fucked or licked. From the looks of things, I was going to be stuck for a while only getting her licked, since a bitch's dick was gone. I was not about to fuck these niggas out here in the streets. They got too many diseases now days. Given the high HIV rate in the city, I was cool. I'd just let a bitch suck on my pussy, or I'd play with myself and be content.

I put on a pink sundress decorated with blue flowers. I grabbed my white LV sandals, and slid my feet in them. My nails and toes were already done in a pink that matched my dress. I grabbed my pink LV purse, got in my red Bentley coupe and headed down- town.

I was thinking of what I would say to Keith to change his mind. When I got to the jail there was a long line of people waiting to see their people. I sat in the car and played with my phone until the line went down. I wasn't about to stand out there in the hot sun getting sweaty, having my pussy and body get smelly and sticky. I was trying to look good for my man.

I got out of the car when there were only three people left in line. I walked over to the guard booth and showed the bored attendant my driver's license.

"Who you here to see," the attendant asked.

"Keith Washington."

The dark, chubby chick looked at a list on the table. "Okay," she said and returned my license.

I was nervous as hell walking down the pink hallway, looking through the glass as I tried to find Keith.

I entered the last booth and sat down on the pink iron stool. A few minutes later, Keith came in. He was wearing a blue sweat suit that had "Federal Inmate." written on the shirt and pants in white letters. His hair was freshly cut, and he looked good, like he had been working out. He sat down, smiled, and picked up the phone.

I was nervous as hell. I had butterflies running through my stomach and my armpits were sweaty. I smiled at him as I picked up the phone. I was as happy as a high school girl on her first date with a boy she had a crush on.

We stared at each other in a daze. After a few seconds, we held our hands together on the glass separating us.

"I love you," he said.

"I love you back."

It took everything in me not to cry right in front of him, but I had to stay strong. I didn't need him to see me cry right in front of him. He was already dealing with enough stress with this fucking case. I wasn't trying to add to it.

"How you been doing?" I asked.

"You know me. This ain't nothing for a stepper."

"I put a thousand dollars on your books."

"Thanks. How are the kids holding up?"

"They're fine."

"And you?"

"l'm trying to be strong, but I'm missing you like crazy."

"I can see in your face that you've been stressing."

"Baby, I ain't going to lie to you. I've been missing you. It's driving me crazy knowing these people can give you a life sentence, and I'll never be with you again."

"Bay, it's going to be all right."

"Stop telling me that shit. You're lying to me. It's not going to be all right. You're are looking at a life sentence. Our kids don't have a father. I'm lying to them every day about where you are at. And you don't want to tell on this guy whoever he is."

"Let me tell your ass something. You always want me to tell on the plug? Let me tell you what's going to happen when I do. He's going to kill your mother. He will kidnap and kill our kids. Then, he will send his men after us and kill your ass and mine. So, what do you want to do now since you got all the motherfucking answers?"

I broke down and cried. "I don't know what the fuck to do. I know all this shit is fucked up, and I'm fucking tired.

I dropped the phone and ran from the jail.

***

Keith

I sat at the phone for a minute with my heart hurting and a few tears falling from my face. I wondered what the fuck had just happened. My heart was hurting for her because I knew she loved me. She was trying to be strong for me.

I wiped my face as I returned to my dorm. I went straight to my cell. I lay in the bed thinking about my wife and kids as my head and heart ached. I knew I was in a fucked up position. I knew what Deloso was capable of. I was not about to put my family through that. They would be better off with me out the way. I was going to have to take one for the team. I had money put up for a rainy day. I couldn't put them in danger for my bullshit from my past. My kids would understand when they're older that I was a G. I had to do what I had to do.

As for Shantell, she was either going to ride or fall after a while. I was not expecting her to put her life on hold for me. I wanted her to move on and be happy, even if it was not with me. All I needed was for her to know I loved her, and I was doing this to keep her and the kids safe.

No matter how much respect I had on the streets, I'd lose it if I turned into a rat. Besides, I just didn't have enough firepower to go up against the whole cartel.

I got out of bed and walked to my partner who was holding our cell phones. He was paying a C.O. to bring us the stuff in.

"What's up, Steve?"

"What's good?" He was sitting on the bed smoking a blunt.

"Nigga, I need you to get me my phone."

"I got you."

He walked to the bathroom showers and retrieved the phone from the stash in the wall.

I went back in the cell and put my blanket up in the doorway like I was about to take a shit. With the camera blocked, I dialed Shantell's number. I needed to get things right with her and let her know I loved her, and I appreciated everything she did for me and the kids.

**

I jumped in the car, crying as I pulled off. I knew it was fucked up the way I just got up and ran off, leaving him there. But I wanted to let him know how I was feeling out here. I knew he loved me, and he would give me and the kids the world.

Shit, he gave us everything.

I knew I shouldn't be mad. Living the way we did came with a price, but damn. I never thought it would be his life. I would give up all this shit for him to be free and here with me.

My phone rang. It was Keith on the cell phone he made me send some man a thousand dollars to get. I picked it up after wiping off my face. I answered the phone.

"Hey, baby girl, I love you."

"I love you too."

"I'm sorry if I made you mad. That's not my intention. I appreciate everything you do for me and the kids. I thank you for holding me down while I'm going through this because I know you don't have to. You do it because you love me. I just want you to know that I want y'all safe. And if you can't stay down with me, it's cool. I don't want you to put your life on hold for me."

"Stop that shit right now. Stop talking fucking stupid. I don't care if they give you a life sentence. I'm going to be there for you. Even if we got to come up with a plan to break you out of that motherfucker. No man can fill your shoes. You give me and the kids everything in the world. I couldn't ask for a better husband, friend, lover, and father for my kids. I'm going to be there for you. I promise you that. No matter what. I love you forever and a day.

"I love you more."

"And I'm going to be in the courtroom every day of your trial to look that bitch ass nigga in the face. I wish I knew where they were keeping him. I would shoot that bitch in the face myself."

"I feel you. I love you. It's about count time, so I got to get off the phone. I'm going to hit you up later tonight."

"Love you."

We hung up. I wanted to be mad at him, but I couldn't. I love him too much. I just have to put on my big girl pants and get ready for a long ride. I hoped they had conjugal visits because a bitch was going to need some dick.

I grabbed the blunt from the ashtray and lit it. I inhaled deeply. Ke'shon turned me on to her weed man. I'd been scoring an ounce of Purp every week. It has helped with my nervous and all the stress I've been through for the last few months. They needed to legalize this weed shit in all fifty states. I keow for sure it would bring down the violence in the fucking states. Motherfuckers would be so high that all they would want to do is smoke, eat, and fuck. Motherfuckers would be on some chill shit. I could promise you that.

Robert Baptiste

Chapter 10

Shantell
Six months later
Sentencing day

I woke up this morning a nervous wreck. I jumped out of bed thinking it was Keith's sentencing day. The day the fucking Feds were going to take my husband away for a long time.

The Feds had been fucking with me the last few months. They were trying to take my shop away. They said Keith paid for it with drug money. But I told Baldwin, and he got in their asses. Now they were leaving me alone about it

I decided to wear my white Prada dress with the cut in the back. I grabbed a part of white open toe stiletto boots. My hair, nails, and toes were done. I sprayed Beyonce perform on then found a white thong and matching bra that had my titties sitting up right.

I looked in the mirror and liked what I saw. I loved the way the dress had my ass sitting right. "Damn, bitch you look good," I said to the mirror.

The weather had turned a little cool in the Fall, so I grabbed my white Prada clutch and got in my white Mercedes G Wagon. As I drove down the interstate, I thought about Keith's trial. I couldn't believe they had found him guilty. Thanks to that bitch ass nigga Dave. That shit still had me in my feelings.

"The United States calls Dave Green to the stand," the ADA announced. I watched the bitch ass nigger walk from the back dressed in a blue suit. I couldn't believe this motherfucker. He was our kids' godfather. He used to sleep at our house. I cooked for him. One time, when he came in broke, Keith looked out for him, and helped him get back on his feet.

And this is how he repaid us. By shitting on our family and taking from our kids.

I swear my blood pressure was rising. I was boiling on the inside. If I had a gun, I would've shot him in the head. They could give me a life sentence along with my husband.

The thin, white ADA looked like Bill Gates. He began with the questions. "Could you tell the jury who the leader of the Calliope Murder gang in New Orleans was?"

Dave pointed at Keith, "Keith Washington." That bitch ass nigga was so scared that he didn't even want to look Keith in the face.

"How many people did you kill for Washington?"

"Around twenty."

"You were one of his primary associates?"

"Yes."

"Was Mr. Washington ever in possession of cocaine in your presence?"

"How much cocaine was in these shipments?"

"Between two to five thousand kilos."

"No further questions."

Baldwin stood up.

"You're doing this to save yourself, right?"

"Objection!" the ADA shouted.

"Overruled, answer the question Mr. Green," the judge answered.

"No, I'm doing it because it's the right thing to do."

"So this has nothing to do with the FBI arresting you with five hundred kilos of cocaine? You're saying this has nothing to do with a deal for less time in exchange for testifying against my client?"

"No."

"Was Mr. Washington still involved with your gang when he was arrested?"

He looked at the prosecutor.

"Answer the question," the judge ordered.

"No, he was not."

Later, the judge dismissed the jury. I clearly remembered the jury returning. I sat on the edge of my seat praying to God that they didn't find him guilty. The trial has lasted three days. The prosecution called fifty witness. Niggas even came from federal prison to point Keith out and identify him as the king pin. They were trying to get their time cut, but Dave's testimony was the one that hurt him most because he had been his righthand man.

"Has the jury reached a decision?" the judge asked.

Caught Up in the Life

"Yes, your honor."

"Proceed."

On the charge of conspiracy to sell cocaine, we find Mr. Washington guilty. On each of the twenty counts of conspiracy to commit capital murder, we find Mr. Washington guilty.

My heart fell to the floor. My head was spinning like I was about to fall out. I left the courtroom. I needed some air badly. I couldn't even think straight. I left court with a headache that lasted a whole week.

Today was going to be even more nerve-racking. I got to the courthouse. I prayed as I went in that the judge would go easy on him. I was prepared to do ten years with him. I could even go to the camp and get some dick. I had heard about women doing that.

I wasn't sure about more time than that.

I walked into a courtroom that was cold as a motherfucker. I got there just as the marshal was bringing Keith from the back. He had on a dark blue jogging suit with "Federal Inmate" written in white down the side of his pants and top of his sweatshirt. He had on a pair of black Air Max tennis shoes. His hair was cut short with waves in it. His beard was trimmed nice and right, just like I liked it.

He smiled at me, and I blew a kiss back at him. He stood at the podium beside Baldwin. The ADA was at the other podium.

"Court is in session. Do either of you wish to present a witness?" the judge asked.

"No, your honor," both Baldwin and the ADA replied.

"Let's get this done then. I've strongly considered giving you a life sentence, Mr. Washington. Yet, it is apparent that you have made a serious attempt to change your life. Because of that, I've decided against a life sentence."

I took a deep breath.

The judge continued, "However, it is undeniable that your actions have led to many problems in New Orleans. Thus, I'm going to sentence you to thirty years. Marshal, please take Mr. Washington back into custody."

"What!" I jumped up screaming. "Thirty fucking years! He didn't do shit! Fuck you bitches. You bitches dead wrong for giving him that much time! What about his fucking family?"

67

"Order!" the judge banged his gavel on the desk.

"Fuck you, you Uncle Tom motherfucker! Fuck you, bitch!"

"Marshal, remove that woman from the court."

The older white marshal tried to grab my arm. I pulled away with fire in my eyes. I walked out of the courtroom with the marshal on my heels. I pointed my middle finger at the judge as I walked out.

I jumped in my car and drove aimlessly around the city, crying my eyes out. Thirty years. I couldn't fucking believe it.

I wanted to get my kids from mother's house, but I did not feel like hearing the bullshit from my mother. I wasn't in the mood for it. Besides, I didn't want my kids to see me with my eyes bloodshot red and me a complete emotional wreck.

At home, I went straight to bed and fell in it completely dressed. I was balling up and crying. It felt like I was dying inside. I must have fallen asleep. My phone woke me up, and I noticed it was six pm. It was Keith. I took a deep breath and prepared myself to hear the bullshit.

"Man, where you been? I've been calling you all day."

"I came home and cried myself to sleep. I didn't hear the phone ringing."

"What was that shit in court today?"

"I don't know. I was mad as a motherfucker."

"Yeah, but going off wasn't going to change shit."

"You should be mad too."

"Shit. I am, but going off wasn't going to make a difference. I'm glad he didn't give me life."

"Shit, he might as well. Thirty years just like it."

"Baldwin filed an appeal."

"Shit, that might take years."

"I don't need extra stress on my ass. I need you to be in my corner."

"I'm in your corner, but you got to understand where I'm coming from. I'm stressing too. I'm out here with two kids I got to raise on my own while my husband's in prison for thirty fucking years."

"I feel you, Shantell, but I can't do anything about it."

"How about tell on them people."

"And when I do, where we going to live? See you're not street. You don't really understand who I'm tied in with. I'm part of something big: the fucking Gulf Coast Cartel. I'm sorry you found out about my past life like this, but it is what it is. I can't tell on the cartel, but you and the kids going to be straight. I promise you that."

"I got to go. I love you."

"Love you back."

I got off the phone feeling worse than I did before. "Trust him, he said. Nigga, you tripping. I got two kids to raise by myself while your ass is in prison for thirty years."

I figured I was going crazy since I was talking to myself. I grabbed a whole bottle of Patron from the bar and took it to the bathroom. I lit candles while running a hot bubble bath. I put a Keith Sweat C.D. in the player, blasting it.

I got in the tub, hitting my blunt and sipping tequila. I was trying to figure out how I was going to move on without Keith. Eventually, I gave up. I got out of the tub and grabbed my phone in the bedroom to call Icy.

I needed to relieve some stress. And what better way to do it when you can't get no dick than to get your pussy and asshole ate out?

Icy answered the phone. "What you doing?" I asked.

"Nothing... just chilling at the house."

"You want to come over for some fun?"

"I'm on my way."

"See you in a minute."

I put on lotion, changed the music, and pulled out a few of my toys. Thirty minutes later, she rang the doorbell. Icy had on light blue shorts that had her pussy and ass hanging out. She wore a white halter that showed off her flat stomach and small waist. She had cut her

hair and dyed it red.

"Come in," I hugged her.

"Where Keith at?"

"Not here. It's a long story."

"So, it's just you and me tonight?"

"Yeah." I smiled. "Just us, girl."

We went to the bedroom removing our clothes. I lay back on the bed and spread my legs wide. She went down eating my pussy out. I grinded my pussy in her face as she sucked on my clit.

"Yes, eat my pussy!"

"You taste good," she said raising her head to look at me.

"Bitch, you like the way I taste, huh?"

"Yes."

I came hard in her mouth, shaking all out of control. I held her head down as she licked it all up. She turned me over and spread my ass cheeks. She ate my ass out like groceries. This caused me to come some more.

I returned the favor, eating her the same way. We sixty-nined each other, cuming in each other's mouth.

She put on my strap on, slammed it in, and fucked the shit out of me. I dug my nails in her back as she slammed the black nine-inch rubber dick in and out of me as I came back to back. I did her the same way to let her get off. We lay there after climaxing back to back.

Then I turned over and started crying.

"What's wrong? Why're you crying?"

"I'm sorry. It had nothing to do with you. I've been an emotional wreck for months."

"So, let's talk about it."

I faced her in the bed. I did need to talk to somebody about this. "I've been stressing a lot lately. I got a whole lot on my plate."

"What's going on?"

I took a deep breath. People say it helps to talk to someone who's not part of the problem. I sure hoped they were right. "Keith's in jail."

"For what?"

"A lot of shit. They gave him thirty years today."

"Damn, I'm sorry. If you need me, I'm here."

"Thanks." Tears were streaming down my face.

She pulled me to her, and we lay in the bed just holding each other.

Chapter 11

Shantell

After getting up and showering, my phone rang. Icy had left a few hours ago. I was feeling a bit better.

The phone rang, and I answered it.

"Baby, they about to move me," Keith said.

"Do you know where at?"

"Beaumont Tx. To the USP."

"I'll send money when you get there."

"I'll call when I make it."

"Love you."

"Love you more."

I put on some tight blue jeans with a white Bebe shirt and some with red and white Air Max. I grabbed my white Nike hat and left the house. I had an appointment with Jackie to get my hair fixed, and God knows I needed it.

As I started driving, my phone rang. I answered.

"Hello."

"Bitch! Where you at?"

"I'm on the way."

"Bitch, you was supposed to be here thirty minutes ago. I gave your appointment to somebody else."

"Jackie, bitch, don't play with me right now. I need my shit done."

"I'm playing. Got you when you get here."

"I'll be there in five."

"See you."

I pulled up to Jackie's red brick duplex. She lived in one half and did hair in the other. The one thing I didn't like about it was it was in the middle of the hood. Bunker Hill was a real trap spot where niggas be hustling and shooting at one another. You named it, they did it around here. As a matter of fact, this was where I met Keith. Little did I know, but he was running all the dope around here.

I walked in her house. It didn't smell like anything but weed and hairspray. Bitches were laughing, and talking about the niggas they fucked, who had the most money, and who ran the city. These bitches were straight hood.

I hugged Jackie.

"Bitch, you going to be next."

"All right." I went and sat down.

Jackie was one of my best friends. We'd been kicking it since a friend of ours introduced us fifteen years ago. Jackie was a straight hood bitch. She stripped and did hair. The bitch was thick like government cheese with a little waist and big fake ass. She looked like Yandy from *Love and Hip Hop.* Her long hair was in blue and red waves down to her ass. She knew about everything going on in the streets and didn't get involved in relationship. She had a couple of niggas to trick off with and pay her bills.

I sat on the sofa listening to these hood bitches talking shit about who they were fucking and who was balling in the streets. A lot of these hoes in here didn't like me. They found out Keith was my husband. They were trying to fuck him, and he turned their bump ass down. A few of these thirsty ass hoes were his side pieces, and he let them go when he started fucking me.

"Come on, Shantell," Jackie said.

I sat in her chair looking at my hair in the mirror. "I want it cut short. Like Toni Braxton used to wear her shit."

"I got you. What's up with Keith?"

"They moving him to Beaumont USP."

"Bitch, I heard they call that motherfucker Bloody Beaumont. Every time you look around they finding a dead body in there or a motherfucker getting stabbed up."

"I ain't worried. Keith knows how to handle himself."

"So, you going to stay down or what?"

"Yeah, bitch. That's my husband."

As I was talking, I saw this red bitch looking in my mouth, rolling her eyes at me. She used to be one of Keith's side pieces. The bitch lied and said Keith was her baby daddy. Come to find out some other nigga was the baby daddy. The hoe was so thirsty for Keith that she lied like that.

"Hold up, bitch in my mouth," I said.

"Who?" Jackie asked.

"This red, thirsty bitch that used to fuck with Keith. Bitch, what you looking at?" I stood up.

The whole shop got quiet, and bitches went to looking at who I was talking to. She stood up.

"Nah, you hoes ain't going to cut up in here today. Tarnika leave. Come back in an hour," Jackie ordered.

I watched her ass walk out the door. I sat down in the chair. "Stupid, thirsty bitch."

"Child, don't let her work on your nervous. Now, how much did he get?"

"Thirty fucking years."

"Bitch, What? And you're going to stay with him? I'd been left his ass."

"Bitch. That's my husband. I'm still in love with him. It's just not that easy to leave."

"Better you than me. Because a bitch like me need D-I-C-K in her life."

"Don't you have a man in jail?"

"Bitch. When that nigga got them ten years, bitch, I was out. It's over. I ain't got time be staying down with no nigga in jail. The only thing I do with a nigga out of prison is fuck them if they got some good dick. Other than that, they on their own."

"You a coldblooded bitch. I can't do that. I'm married to my dick for better or worse. I got two kids with Keith."

"I feel you. To each his own. Married or not, his ass is out. I'll send him money and shit. I ain't doing all the visiting and writing shit. He's fucking dead to me. He better have his side bitch hold him down."

"Bitch, you right not to be in a relationship or getting married."

"Bitch, I know that's right. I ain't going to do right anyway. I'm a hoe. I like to fuck different niggas and get money outta them. They get them, and I get me. We both get what we want."

"Bitch, when are you going to get a real shop?"

"Bitch, when you give me some of them millions you and Keith got over there."

"Bitch, I might invest with you in a shop."

"You need to... We done."

I looked in the mirror and smiled, "I like it. I handed her a hundred dollar bill.

"Thanks."

We hugged. "I'll call you later."

"All right."

***

I left Jackie's house to pick up the kids from school. We went and got ice cream. I needed to spend some time with them. I'd had so much shit on my plate I hadn't spent any time with them. I knew they were going to ask questions about their father, especially Kawine because she loved her some Keith.

As we sat at the park Kawine turned and looked at me. "Mama, when is my daddy coming home?"

I wanted to cry but I held back my tears back. I couldn't tell them he'd never be home. It would crush them to know he choose the streets over them. I hated lying to my kids, but I felt in my heart they were too young to understand.

So, I lied. "He'll be home soon. He had to take a job in China."

"Can we go see him in China?" Keith, Jr asked.

"Not right now, but soon."

"Okay, can we talk to him on the phone? I want to tell him about all the A's I'm getting in school."

"Sure, we'll have to wait for him to call. Now, eat your ice cream, so we can go."

As we were getting up, the phone rang. "You got a prepaid call from Keith Washington."

I quickly pushed five on my phone.

"Hey, baby. What's going on?"

"Nothing. Just took the kids to get some ice cream."

"Baby, I need you to tell them where I'm at."

"Keith, they are seven and eight. They're not really for that. Don't tell them. I'll tell them when the time is right."

"You know I hate lying to my kids."

"I know, but please do it for me. I'll put them on the phone. Look, I told them you are in China, so stick to that. Okay? I love you."

"I got it, but we have to talk about it."

"Here's the kids. Kids, your daddy is on the phone."

Kawine grabbed my phone, smiling. "Hey, daddy, I miss you. When you coming home?"

"Soon. I love you."

"Love you too."

"Let me talk to your bother,"

"Her, Keith Jr."

"Hey, daddy, when you coming home?"

"I'll be back soon."

"Okay, I love you."

"I love you too, I need you to watch out for your sister and mother for me, okay?"

"Okay, daddy. I love you."

"Put you mother on the phone."

"Here mom."

"The phone is about to hang up. 1'll call you later. Love you."

"Love you more."

When we got back to the house Federal Agents were everywhere. They had the cars on a wrecker. What the fuck is going on? These bitches already got my husband. What else do they want?

"Kids stay in the car. I'll be right back."

I walked over to a bald, black agent wearing a dark blue US Marshal jacket

"What's going on?"

"Mrs. Washington, how are you?"

"Not fucking good. Why are y'all taking my shit?"

"Go talk to Agent Sims. He's in charge." He pointed to a bald white guy.

"Excuse me," I said as I walked over to him."

"Mrs. Washington?"

"Yes."

"Here's an eviction notice and repossession note for the attached property."

"Y'all can't do this."

"We're the government. We can do what we want. Especially since your husband used proceeds from drug sales to buy it."

"What about my kids? Where are we supposed to live?"

"We have to let you have two weeks before eviction, so you have time to find another house. We seized your husband's construction company and froze your joint bank accounts."

"I have kids. How am I supposed to feed them?"

"That's not my problem. We will notify you when we finish the investigation as to whether any property will be returned."

I wanted to slap the fuck out of him. I swear I did. "We'll see about this shit." I walked off mad as a

motherfucker. I called Baldwin. "Baldwin, these motherfuckers are at my house taking all my shit. They froze all the bank accounts and took Keith's company."

"Okay, we knew that would happen when they convicted Keith of selling drugs. They can take anything in his name."

"The fucking house is in both our names."

"They can seize anything with his name on it."

"What am I supposed to do? I got fucking kids."

"I'll look into it."

"Thanks."

I got the kids from the car and took them in the house. I watched as those bitches took eleven of our cars and trucks. I sat down on the couch shaking my motherfucking head. What the fuck is going on in my life? How did it get all fucked up? All because a bitch ass nigga ratted on my husband.

The phone rang. It was the person I most needed to talk to. "You got a prepaid call from Keith Washington."

"Hey, baby, what's up?"

"Shit is all fucked up."

"What's wrong now?"

"The Feds took everything. They're giving me two weeks to sell my shit and get the fuck out the house. They froze all the bank accounts with your name on them, I have just enough money to feed the kids and me. I need money to pay bills, and where are we going to stay? Keith, tell me that."

"It's going to be all right. Let me make a call."

"Okay. Love you."

"Love you back."

I made dinner. After we finished eating, I helped the kids with their homework and got them to bed.

***

I got up the next morning to the doorbell ringing. The kids didn't have to go to school. It was Martin Luther King Day. To my surprise the kids were asleep.

I looked through the peephole and saw the mailman. I fixed my robe and opened the door, "Yes?"

"Mrs. Washington?"

"Yes."

"Sign here."

I signed the paper, took the package from his hand and closed the door. On the couch, I opened the package. Stacks of money wrapped in rubber bands fell out. There was nothing else in the package. It looked like a lot of money

I looked up at the sky. Thank you, God.

I fixed the kids breakfast, and went to soak in a hot bubble bath, As I relaxed the phone rang.

"Bay, you got it right?" Keith said.

"Yes, baby, thank you."

"Take that and put it down on another house."

"How much is it?"

"Seventy five thousand."

"You got more?"

"Don't worry about that. Just take care of you and the kids."

"Okay,"

"What cars did they leave?"

"My Bentley and G Wagon."

"I got to go. The C.O. is making rounds. I need to hide the cell phone. Call you later. Love you."

"Love you back."

"By the way, you're clear to come see me. I need you to handle something for me. I'll tell you when you get here." He quickly disconnected.

Chapter 12

Shantell
Two weeks later

I'm riding down I-10 heading to Beaumont, Texas to see my husband. It was certainly something I never thought I'd do. I was still trying to adjust to my new way of living. I put half the money down on a 2500 square foot house. It was much smaller than I was used to, but it was just down the street from my old house on Lake Forest. It's three bedrooms. It's nice, but not what a bitch is used to.

The Feds returned one of the accounts. It had a few hundred thousand in it, but not like Keith's accounts that had millions. So, now a bitch got to live on a budget. No more big shopping sprees and vacations spent in presidential suites. A bitch got to manage her lifestyle now.

I still heard the bullshit from my mother. She loved to tell me that she told me so, and that I was stupid for sticking by his side. I didn't care. He was my husband, and I was not going to leave him when he was down. I was a ride or die bitch for real. What kind of chick would I be if I ran out on a man who gave me everything? I hadn't even had to work in ten years. I just opened my shop because I was bored for real. So that leave him shit was fucked up. I was supposed to run and leave him on stuck. Fuck that. That was not how I was built,

I pulled into the prison parking lot. It looked like a big castle with a forty foot cement wall around it with a double fence encircling it as well. There was a truck patrolling the perimeter. Security was tight around here. These motherfuckers made sure a motherfucker didn't escape from here.

I got out of the car and look around. There were a bunch of guard towers filled with armed guards. I had heard stories about this place from hoes at Jackie's shop who said they visited niggas here. They said they called it bloody Beaumont because of all the inmates' death here. Even guards were getting stabbed and killed. They said it stayed on lock down.

I prayed to God that nothing would happen to Keith in here or that he wouldn't have to kill a motherfucker and get life. I hoped his appeal comes through and he comes home. I missed him so much. I even slept in one of his old shirts, so I could smell him.

I walked through the double glass doors and saw a slim white chick with long blonde hair. She was wearing a dark blue correctional officer's uniform. "Can I help you, ma'am," she asked.

"I'm here to visit Keith Washington."

"ID."

I gave her my driver's license. She looked at the paper in front of her. "Wait over there with the others."

I sat in blue chair, looking at this group of people anxious to see their loved ones. Five minutes later, the blonde walked over. "Y'all come with me."

She made us walk through a metal detector. I had to remove my shoes and let her run my purse through separately. Me and my little group followed her to the visitation room. She handed our ID's to a slim black chick with long, gold weave in her hair and a lot of make-up on her face. There were blue plastic chairs sitting side by side, a couple of snack machines, and a TV hanging in the corner.

In about twenty minutes Keith came in. He was wearing pressed khaki pants and shirt and a pair of black Timberland boots. His hair was cut low and his waves were banging. His beard was trimmed just liked I like it. He looked like he had been working out. His arms were bigger and more ripped. His face had that prison glow. I was so turned on. I wanted to fuck him right then and there. My pussy was on fire soaking wet.

We hugged and kissed the entire five minutes they allowed. He smelled and felt so good. As we kissed, I was coming on myself. I couldn't lie I didn't want to let him go. That was how I know I still loved him. I had butterflies in my stomach and my pussy was soaking wet. Just like the first time we met. I wanted to cry but didn't. I didn't want him to see me break weak.

"Hey, baby, I love you and miss you." I was smiling like a high school girl with her crush.

"I miss you and love you too. Let's go sit down."

80

I wasn't going to lie. I was nervous as hell. I kept touching him. I couldn't believe it was real. I really was face to face with him without a glass window. I hadn't been able to touch him in a long time. I rubbed his face and kissed him again.

"So, how're you doing?"

"I'm okay. Missing you though."

"I miss you too. How are the kids?"

"Getting big. They miss you too."

"I miss them. You got to bring them to see me."

"I know. I just got to build myself up to tell them."

"What's up with your mother? I know she having a field day with this shit."

"Yeah, she's still on my fucking line about this shit."

"I figured that."

"How your appeal coming?"

"I haven't heard shit yet."

"Keep me posted."

"Got you."

"Do you want something from the snack machine?"

"Some chicken wings and a coke."

"Okay."

I walked over to the machines. Something told me to look back. Sure enough he was looking at my ass. I smiled at him. I was wearing tight black jeans that had my ass sitting up right and a black Gucci blouse with matching loafers. My hair and nails were done. I had my nails done in blue, which was his favorite color.

I walked back and gave him food.

"I see you ass got fatter," he said, smiling.

"For real. I haven't even paid any attention."

"I like it. Your hair looks good too."

"Thanks."

"So, you gave a nigga that ass. He got it nice and right."

"No nigga is fucking this pussy. This still your pussy and ass. I fucked with Icy a couple times but as for a nigga, hell no."

"I was just checking. You know there some sick niggas out there. I'm not saying not get some. I'm just saying be careful."

"I got you."

"Let's go take some pictures."

As we were taking pictures, I felt his dick getting hard on my ass. I leaned back, letting him rub it against my ass. It felt so good. I wished I could jerk him. I let my hand touch it for a second.

"Fuck, I miss it," I said.

"Let's go sit down. I need to talk to you for a second."

We went back to the blue chairs. Suddenly his face turned serious, "I need a favor from you."

"Whatever you need."

"I need you to bring a couple of grams of heroin in here."

"Man, you tripping. Baby, they got this shit on lock down around here. How am I supposed to get that shit in here?"

"In your pussy."

"Keith, you tripping."

"Look, I need it because books of stamps is your money in here."

"I put money on your books."

"It's different on the inside. The stamps is what makes shit move in here."

"What if I get busted?"

"You won't."

'Are you sure?"

"Yes, as long as you do what I say."

"Okay, where do I get this shit from?"

"I got a partner. I'll tell you the rest on the phone later."

"I gotta think about this, because if I get busted…"

"You're not. I promise."

The C.O. came over and told us our visit was over. We hugged and kissed.

"I love you," he said.

"Love you back. I'll be here next weekend."

"Tell the kids I love them too. I'm going to call you."

"All right, I love you."

I went straight to the car. When I got in, I let all my emotions out. I cried hard as a motherfucker. I missed my man so much. I wished I could break him out of that motherfucker.

As soon as I got back to the city, his friend called. "Is this Shantell, Keith's wife?"

"Yes."

'My name is Brad. He told me to holla at you."

"Let's meet at Lakeside Mall in thirty minutes."

"Okay."

I soon pulled up to the mall in the eastern part of New Orleans. A dark skinned, tall man who looked like Dwight Howard got out of a red Benz and walked over to my car and got in.

"Here you go. This a few dollars for him. Tell him I said to keep his head up."

"Okay."

He jumped out of my car. I pulled off nervous as fuck. I hid the plastic bag between my legs. I looked in my rearview the whole way home.

After I got home, Keith called me. "You straight? Did he give it to you?"

"Yeah, we good."

"Love you."

"Love you back."

I walked in the bedroom with my nerves all fucked up. I lit up a blunt and smoked it to calm down. I needed to really think about what Keith wanted me to do. Damn, a bitch was down for her man, but this nigga was really testing a bitch's loyalty. I hit the blunt again.

***

one week later

I was nervous as hell standing in this line to go inside a Federal prison with a pussy full of dope. I guess a bitch would do anything for her husband. I was going to tell his ass I wouldn't do this shit no more. I must've been out my motherfucking mind doing this shit now.

I really loved this man. I'd be glad when this shit was over, so he could come home and help a bitch with these bad ass kids and give me some long overdue loving. A bitch needed some dick in her life badly.

The pussy licking shit was cool, but it was nothing compared to a man's touch and a hard, warm dick in your pussy.

I didn't know how long I could do this. I knew we got married for better or worse but damn a bitch had needs. I loved my husband. I truly did, but this jail shit was weighing on a bitch.

I still hadn't told the kids where Keith was at. They thought he was working overseas. Even though my mom had been bitching, she'd been a trooper with the kids. A few of my friends told me I was stupid for waiting for a man for thirty years, but I didn't pay them any attention. Those hoes had never been married and probably never would be.

"Who're you here to see?" the chunky, black lady asked.

"Keith Washington."

She checked the list for my name. "Go stand over there with the others."

Twenty minutes later, I saw Keith again. We kissed.

"You got it?"

"Yes."

"Okay, go in the bathroom and put them in the trash can."

"Okay."

I walked to the trash can. I was nervous as fuck as I hunted for a camera. I went to the stall, sat on the toilet, and pissed them out. As I walked out, I dropped the bags in to the trash. I went back to the visitation room and tried to look calm as I sat down next to Keith. "We all good," I said.

"Thanks, baby. I love you."

"Don't thanks baby me. I ain't doing that shit no more. I got two kids to think about. If my ass get busted, who would take care of them.

"I'm sorry. You're right. I thought about making some money in here. Sending you some would help."

"Keith, I appreciate you trying to help us out, but I don't need you getting into any bullshit in here. I need you to win your appeal and get out. I'm already worried about you in here with all the fucking stabbings I heard about."

"You don't have to worry. I got this on the inside."

"I know you can handle yourself. It's just the wife in me that worries about you."

"Okay, how are the kids?"

"Fine. I'll send you some pictures when I get home."

"Shantell, I know you love me, but I know you got needs. You look stressed the fuck out. Go out and have some funny."

"So, what are you saying? Keith? You want me to leave you in here and find another man? I want you."

"Baby, I love you, but it would be selfish of me to ask you to put your life on hold for thirty years."

"I feel where you coming from, but I'm not just going to leave you here. I'm going to be with you every step of the way."

"That's why I love you."

"Keith, you don't know. It hurt me to my soul every time I come in and see you in here. Then I got to leave you in here. I cry in my car every time I leave this fucker."

"Baby, I'm sorry all this happened. I didn't mean for it to happen. I didn't think my past would come back years later and fuck me like this."

"I know you didn't."

"I'm truly sorry I hurt you and the kids."

"I know." I leaned in and kissed him. I lay back in his arms, and we just watched T.V. until the C.O. announced that the visit was over.

"Tell the kids I miss them."

"Will do."

I got in my Bentley and cried my eyes out like I always did when I leave him here. It felt like a part of me was being torn out. As I pulled out of the parking lot, Jackie called me.

"What's up, bitch? You still coming?"

"I don't know."

"What's wrong with you? Are you coming from seeing Keith again?"

"Yeah," I said through tears.

"I don't know why you keep putting yourself through this stress. Just leave his ass and move on."

"It's just not that easy when you're still in love, Jackie?"

"Look, I got a way for you to get Keith out of prison."

"Bitch! Don't play with me right now."

"I'm dead ass serious."

"I'm coming to you house in a few hours." I sure hoped this bitch was not playing with me right now.

I finally got to her house. She answered the door barefoot with hot pink boy shorts and a white wifebeater on. She was smoking a blunt, and music was blasting from the back. I walked in, taking the joint and hitting it as I went by. "You got something to drink?"

"Yeah, something strong."

She came back with vodka and shot glasses. She poured us two shots each, and we hit them back to back.

"Now tell me this great fucking plan to get my man out of prison, and it better not be no bullshit."

"It's not no bullshit. Remember that nigga, Boo? The one I used to fuck with?"

"Yeah, that nigga was hustling."

"Well his ass went to the Feds for two bricks and got fifteen years."

"Bitch, what that got to do with me?"

"Bitch, if you listen, I will tell you."

"Pass the blunt. I'm listening."

"I was in love with the nigga. I ain't going to lie. The nigga put it down on me. He worked out a deal with the prosecutor. I set niggas up, and he get his time cut."

"Did it work?"

"Hell, yeah. I set up a couple of niggas out of town, and they cut his sentence in half, but they gave him all the credit."

"You still fuck with him?"

"Fuck no. That dumb ass nigga went back to prison on a gun case. He got ten years. I'm just saying you can cut a deal with the prosecutor and get Keith's time cut. He'll be home earlier than thirty years."

"How sure are you it will work for me?"

"Bitch, the Feds are going to let you know when you ask them?"

"All right, bitch, Now pass me that blunt."

I left Jackie's house fucked up. Once home, I went straight to bed and lay across it. I thought about what Jackie had said. I was fucked up over it at first. It was just like what Dave did to Keith, and he got thirty years. Now I wanted to do the same thing? I had to think long about it.

Caught Up in the Life

Next thing I knew, I was knocked out on the bed.

***

Early the next morning, I was still thinking about it. I jumped into a hot shower and let the hot water run over my body. I took the time to please myself. It was overdue. It had been a couple of months since me and Icy had gotten together, plus I was stressed the fuck out. I came so hard I almost fell down.

I got out, dried off, and put on my Saint Laurent jean dress with matching high heel sandals. I fixed myself in the mirror and grabbed my purse and left. I went to the Federal building on camp street. I had made up my mind. Motherfuckers didn't care if they broke up my happy home. Why should I care about the next motherfucker's home? I knew it was selfish, but I had to do what I had to do to get my man home.

I took a deep breath, went into the building and headed straight to the prosecutor's office. We had spoken on the phone, so he was expecting me. Even better, the prosecutor was the same one who helped Jackie. I had made up my mind. I needed my man at home.

I knocked on the glass office door.

"Come in."

I walked in the office. He was behind a long wooden desk that was covered with paperwork. He stood, and we shook hands.

"Have a seat. What can I do for you?"

"I'm trying to get my husband out of prison."

"Do you really understand what you're asking?"

"Yes, sir, my friend Jackie said you helped her out on a case.

I remember Ms. Waters. How is she doing?"

"Crazy as always. Let's get down to business."

"Well, this is what we do. We send you on a few stings and every arrest knocks time off Mr. Washington's sentence."

"Okay, how many people do I got to bust?"

"A lot. Mr. Washington got thirty years. We'll call you in a couple of days."

I left feeling fucked up. I signed on with the motherfucker who put my man in prison to put more motherfuckers in prison. But I needed my husband at home, and if this what it took, I was all for it.

Chapter 13

Shantell

On my first mission for the Feds, I was nervous as hell. They made me dress like a rock head with old clothes and a fucked up wig. They had me wire up. They dropped me off at a place on the outskirts of New Orleans called the dump. It was a hood in Kenner, Louisiana. I walked to a white house on the corner. A bunch of niggas were there selling crack.

One of the guys stopped me and asked what I wanted. I told him I needed a couple of twenty dollar rocks. He pulled out a bag of rocks showing them to me. I grabbed two and handed him the money. I went back to the van and showed the agents what he sold me.

The next thing I knew the Feds raided the house. They had everyone handcuffed on the ground as they searched the house. They found fifty thousand dollars and two keys of coke. They put everyone in the black van.

Next, they sent me to another spot in Kenner called Shrews Berry where they were hustling heroin. They wanted to clean the hood,

I went to a red and brown house in the middle of the block. A slim, dark-skinned guy with a bald head opened the door. "What you need?"

"Something for a hundred."

"Come in."

I followed him to the back of the house. I saw two women smoking the pipe and shooting up dope as they turned tricks with two guys.

"Damn, you fine," he said, turning to look at me. "You want to fuck instead of giving me money?"

"No, I'm good."

He gave me bags of heroin. As I left, I saw several men and a woman in the kitchen surrounded by dope counting money.

As I reached the front door the Feds rushed in with guns drawn. They made everyone, including me, get on the floor. At first, I was fucked up about what I was doing, but I kept telling myself it was for my husband.

I busted trap houses for the next three weeks. Then it was time for my reward.

"We have a problem." I was in the prosecutor's office.

"What's going on?" I confusedly asked.

"Well, we appreciate you work, but the FDA doesn't want to let you husband out."

"That's not what you told me. When is my man getting out of jail!" I shouted

"Please lower you voice."

"What's the fucking problem?"

"Your husband wasn't just anybody. We can't just let him out of prison. We can take five years off, but he won't go free. Not for drugs and murders. Keith was a gang leader. The FDA won't let him walk."

"What kind of fucking game is this?" I asked getting loud. You told me if I put in this work, my husband was coming home. I risked my motherfucking life for y'all motherfuckers and now you tell me some bullshit."

"Calm down, Mrs. Washington."

"What the fuck you mean calm down? You lied to me."

"I ran it by the boss. He said it was a no go because your husband was a kingpin in the Calliope Murder gang. He says he needs a body for a body."

"That's some bullshit. You know what I'm going to do? I'll go to the newspaper and tell them everything. I'll tell them how y'all use people's family to bust drug dealers. Then you don't give that person credit or keep promises and put families at risk to be killed."

"I know how you feel, but we don't want attention brought to this program. The only way to get your husband out of prison is to get this man." He slid a picture over to me, but I didn't even look at it. I stalked out of the office as he followed trying to talk to me.

"Mrs. Washington, wait. We can really get him out this way."

"Fuck you."

I stormed out the front door. In my car, I grabbed my phone and called Jackie.

"I'm on my way over."

"All right. What's wrong?"

"I'll tell you when I get there."

I flopped down on the sofa, mad and disgusted at the same damn time. She sat next to me and rubbed my back.

"What happened?"

I looked her in the face and wiped my tears away. "I did everything them bitches told me to do, and they still won't let him go."

"What you talking about?"

"I went to see the prosecutor like you told me and cut the deal. I worked like a bitch for three straight weeks straight busting motherfuckers. They promised me they would let him go. Them motherfuckers lied to me."

"So, what they talking about?"

"He told me he needed a body for a body since Keith's is a high-profile case. They want me to help them bust some fool. I don't need no more bullshit."

"What did you say?"

"I didn't say shit. I just looked at him like he was crazy, grabbed my shit, and walked the fuck out of his office cursing him out. I threatened his ass. I told him I was going to talk to the newspapers."

"Bitch, you crazy."

"Bitch, I went off. I need some weed to calm my nerves. You got some?"

"Here, light this blunt up. What are you going to do?"

"I don't know. I saw niggas beat a junky with a baseball bat after he tried to take off with their dope. Another time, this nigga in a trip house, tried to rape me. Good thing the DEA was there to save my black ass."

"Damn, I didn't have to go through all that. I just met a couple of drug niggas and set their ass up. Then, it was over with."

"Bitch, they made me work for mine."

"So, what you going to do? You going to bust the fool they want, or your kids going to be thirty when he gets out? And you going to be old as fuck."

"I don't know, Jackie. I don't know. After those bitches lied to me, I can't trust them anymore. I won't go on any more missions."

"I feel you."

I lay my head on her lap, crying as a million thoughts ran through my head. Just then she turned the T.V. up.

"Bitch, look."

"What?"

"Today a man named Dave Green was murdered outside of a Federal halfway house."

"That's good for that motherfucker. I wish I was the one that did it."

Chapter 14

Shantell

I spent the night at Jackie's house. That morning I got up and dressed, leaving Jackie's ass asleep on the couch.

I jumped in the car with a lot on my mind. I was glad that bitch ass nigga Dave was dead. I wished it happened early. That way he couldn't have testified on Keith. I wished I knew who did it. I would give them some money.

One thing was Keith wanted me to bring the kids to see him. I really wasn't ready for them to see him. I kept telling him we'll see about it. I knew it had been more than three years, but I was afraid for them to go see him,

They would start acting up in school because their father was in prison. Plus, they'd have a thousand questions. Why is their father in jail? When will he be home? I couldn't deal with the looks on their faces when I told them how long his sentence was, and that he won't come home any time soon. I was just not prepared to go through that right now. I couldn't break their hearts. I already had too much stress on my plate.

At home, I found a glass and a bottle of red wine. I took them to the bathroom, ran a hot bubble bath, lit a candle, and got in. I was smoking some weed and sipping the wine.

I sat there crying about my husband. I was an emotional wreck. I didn't know what to do. On one hand, I wanted my man home. On the other, I didn't want to work with those bitches no more.

Sipping wine and hitting the blunt, I let my thoughts roll through my head. My kids needed their father. I needed my husband home, but I wasn't trying to put my family in danger. My daughter needed her father to give her the game on these niggas out in the streets, and Jr needed him because I couldn't show him how to be a man. That was something they needed their father to teach them. A father was important in his kids' lives.

I got out of the tub, lay on the bed butt-naked and continued thinking about my situation. I fell asleep high as a motherfucker, thinking about Keith.

I woke up to my ringing phone. It was the Federal Prosecutor's office I didn't want to answer it. I wasn't ready for their bullshit today. Moreover, I wasn't over the way they used me. After some hesitation, I answered. "What do you want?"

"The FDA wants to make a deal to get your husband out of jail."

"I ain't got no time for bullshit."

"It's not. He's willing to help you. I told him about how you helped us. He just wants to talk."

"I'll be there in an hour."

"See you then."

I got dressed and called Baldwin. I told him to meet me at the federal building on Camp.

***

Baldwin and I sat in the prosecutor's office waiting for the meeting. I had told him everything I did. I made him promise not to tell Keith and promised him a few extra dollars if he kept it between me and him.

Mr. Vance, the FDA, started by giving me a couple of pictures of a Mexican man. He was short, had a medium build, short black hair and a long, big mustache. He was smoking a cigar.

"He look like El Chapa. Who is he?" I asked.

"This is Deloso."

"What do you want me to do?"

"Before getting into that, I want to tell you about him. He's the biggest cartel boss on the Gulf Coast. Everything goes through him. This is who your husband was in bed with. He moved a lot of his product and killed people for him as well."

I finally saw the man the Feds wanted Keith to rat on. He didn't look nearly as dangerous as Keith implied.

"How do I get next to him?"

"The same way your husband did. Sell drugs. Have you seen the film *Deep Cover*?"

94

"Yeah, Larry Fisburne was a cop in it."

"You're now a Federal Agent. What he did is what you're going to do. I do need to warn you. We've lost a lot of agents dealing with this man."

"What you mean... Lost?"

"Their cover was blown. They were killed."

"No disrespect meant, but I don't think I can do this. It was a mistake. I got kids to think about. I'll wait on my husband's appeal. He might get out."

"He won't win. There's too many witnesses to his actions... murders and drug trafficking in New Orleans."

I sat back. I felt like the air had been knocked out of me. I stared at the prosecutor. A million thoughts ran through my mind. Did I really want my husband home so bad that I willing to risk my life to do it?

"I'll do it, but only on two conditions. It has to be in writing. If anything happens to me, Keith still gets out of prison, and he can't find out how he got out."

"Agreed. We can make it look like he won his appeal. There's no need for him to know."

"Where do I sign? I'm going to need some money to buy the cocaine. Being that y'all took all my money, I need some."

He reached in a drawer and removed a check made out to me for $24,000."

"Twenty-four thousand is enough for a kilo of coke. You will report to me only. I'll be with you every step of the way."

"I don't know where to buy cocaine."

"Don't give me that. You lived in the projects until you mother met your stepfather. He was a bigtime dealer in the city. We were trying to bust him. We would have gotten him if he hadn't been killed. You know something about the streets."

"What about my mother and kids?"

"We'll protect them."

I took a deep breath as Baldwin and I signed the agreement. I put the check in my purse. Baldwin and I walked out of the building to my car.

"Shantell, you're beautiful. Call me if you need anything. I'll check on your mother and kids from time to time."

"I appreciate everything you did for me." I hugged him and got in my car,

"It's all good. Be safe."

"I will." I drove off.

On the way home, I tried to think about who I could get a brick from. I thought about asking Jackie, but I just didn't want to score dope from a nigga out of the hood. Next thing you know, he'd be trying to jack a bitch. Then I really would be ass out.

I needed a plug. Someone who really moved bricks. I didn't want a nigga that was going to be on my line, talking about my business and asking a bitch a lot of questions. I didn't need this shit getting back to my husband. I was trying to stay as low key as possible. I just wanted to do this shit and be out.

I needed someone like my husband had. Someone from out of town. As I rode around, I thought about people I knew who were in the game. As I got home, I thought about my best friend from college. I went to Houston with her. She was always in the streets and knew what was going on. She had been in jail. The Feds picked her up for trafficking drugs across state lines. She used to hustle weed back in college to pay our bills. I hadn't seen her in a couple of years. She had come to the house on Fat Tuesday. I wondered if she was still stripping. I hoped she still had the same number. I knew this bitch knew somebody that was moving the work.

I found her number in my phone. It went to the damn voice mail. "This is Dream. Leave a message at the beep."

"Brittney, this is Shantell. I know we ain't spoke in a while, but I need you to hit me back when you can. We need to talk."

I went to the kitchen to make a ham sandwich. I didn't have to cook. The kids were gone to a summer camp for six weeks. Thank God.

As I went back to the bedroom, my phone rang. I hoped it was Brittney, but it was Keith. He had bought a cell phone but could only talk on certain days at certain times.

"Hey, baby," I said.

"Hey, love. What's going on?"

"Nothing. I was just fixing me something to eat. I was waiting for your call. I miss you, and I love you."

"Miss and love you too. Where are the kids?"

"At summer camp."

"Tell them I love them."

"Will do."

"What you got on?" he asked.

"Some tights and a shirt."

"I wish I was there."

"Me too, so, so bad."

"When are you going to send me some pictures?"

"I got you."

"I need some freak ones."

"I'm going to hook you up."

"Hang up, and I'll call you back on Skype. I want to see you play with you pussy."

"All right."

I took off my clothes and put a towel underneath me on the bed. He called me back in thirty seconds. As I picked up the phone, I was looking at him naked on the screen with his dick rock hard in his hand.

I watched him jerk off as I played with my pussy. I eased my finger in and out of my wetness. I got in a doggy-style position and was sticking a finger in my asshole and pussy as I moaned. "Fuck. Jerk that dick. Let me see you cum."

I watched as he started to shake. I put my face close to the screen to watch him about to cum. I pretended he was shooting it all over my face. "That's it, baby. Let it come out. Shoot it."

"Shit," he said, shooting it all over the screen. "Hold on, baby." He left but quickly returned to the phone smiling. "Thanks, baby. I needed that."

"I told you that I got you."

"They about to count. I'll call you later. Love you."

"Love you back."

Shit, I needed that to relieve some stress.

I took pictures of my pussy and asshole. I printed them from the computer along with some recent pictures of kids.

My phone rang. I smiled as I saw it was Brittney. "Hey, stranger," I said.

"What's up, bitch? You don't know me no more since you got married."

"Well, I'm a mother now. I can't hang like I used to."

"Whatever, bitch. "

"I need to talk to you."

"So, talk."

"I can't on the phone. Can I come and see you?"

"Anytime, bitch. I'm stripping."

"I'll be there Friday."

"Alright. Love you."

"Love you back. I'm looking forward to seeing you."

Chapter 15

Shantell

The next morning, I grabbed my LV suitcase and threw in some clothes. I slid on a yellow sundress with a red thong, no bra, and a pair of open-toe white Gucci sandals.

On my way out of town I stopped by my mother's house to tell her where I'd be in case she needed me. My mother was in the kitchen cooking breakfast. She was high yellow, almost white. She was a Creole woman with long, black hair, big ass and breasts and a small waist. She was fifty-five but could pass for a young forty. She still acted young though. All she did was mess with younger men.

"It smells good in here." I kissed her on the cheek.

"Hey, baby, what brings you by?"

"I'm going out of town to see Brittney."

"Don't you mean your used to be lover?"

"No, mom, she wasn't my lover. We just had a few sexual experiences together. I just wanted to give you money in case the kids need it while I'm not around."

"Okay, be safe. Tell Brittney I say hey."

"Will do."

I hit I-10 heading for Houston. I hadn't been to Houston in a while. Brittney and I were roommates for four years in college at the University of Houston. We were both business majors. She always had my back. When my mother sent tuition money, and I would blow it on parties and strip clubs, she gave me extra money. We used to party our asses off night and day.

She was the one who turned me on to liking women. One night, we were chilling at the apartment we were renting. We were smoking weed and drinking, just getting high. She suddenly leaned over and kissed me on the lips. I didn't stop her. She began to tongue kiss me as I kissed her back. She pulled down my boy shorts and started eating my pussy out. I came harder than I ever had before. I had never cum like that with a man, so I returned the favor.

We were never in a relationship. We were just fuck partners. When she went to jail, I met Keith while home on summer vacation. Like they say, the rest is history. I never went back to Houston, but I sent her money when she called. I'd been with Keith ever since.

I pulled out my phone, hitting her up. "Bitch, I'm corning into downtown Houston right now."

"Okay, I'll meet you at Scott Gertner's. It's a sport bar on Fannin."

Shortly, I pulled up to the sports bar. Brittney pulled in behind me in a green Honda Accord sitting on some chrome rims with tinted windows. Even though she was every bit of thirty-three. She looked like she was twenty-one. She was wearing leggings that showed off her coke bottle shape and fake, round ass. She had the same shape in college. Her short shirt showed off her flat stomach and pierced belly ring.

She had some fake, blue hair that hung down to her ass. She was wearing black Prada sandal heal that showed off her pink polished toenails. She favored Porsha from *Real Housewives of Atlanta*.

The crazy thing was that she doesn't even work out. The bitch ate everything.

We hugged and kissed one another. "Bitch! You still look good." I said as I stepped back to look.

"Bitch! I see life treating you good. I see you with the big Benz truck. You look good too."

"Bitch, if you only knew the stress and troubles I've been through."

"Bitch, I hear you. I got my own shit too."

Inside the bar, we sat in a booth. "Can I take ya'll order?" the waitress asked.

"Bring us a couple of strawberry margaritas," Brittney answered."' So, bitch, how has life been treating you?"

"Bitch, life's been kicking my ass."

"What? I thought you were happily married to the man of your dreams with two beautiful kids. That's what you told me last time."

"Bitch, I did. I do. I'm still married with two beautiful kids ... but the man of my dreams is in prison with thirty years."

The waitress brought our drinks.

"Why did Keith get thirty years?"

"This bitch ass nigga got busted and brought Keith's past up to the Feds. He told them he used to work for Keith and did a lot of killing for him."

"Damn, niggas ain't shit these days."

"Tell me about it."

"What do you need me to do?"

"Help me get a brick of coke."

"For what?"

"Bitch, I'm struggling. The Feds took everything. I got two kids. I need to bust a move."

"Bitch, you sitting on a money maker. They have a lot of niggas out here that would break you off. And the strip clubs always hiring."

"Bitch, that's not my get down."

"I'll see what I can do. I still know a few people in the streets." I hated lying to my friend, but I couldn't tell her the truth."

"How long you planning on staying in town?" she asked.

"A week or so."

"Look like we going to party all this weekend like we used to do. You still down with the women?"

"A little bit with my husband. We do it to spice up the relationship."

"Well, you know I got to get some of that one on one action for old times. I got a couple of cuties for us too."

"Well, we'll have to see about that. I'm down here on some business."

"Don't worry about that. We going to make it happen. Right now, we going to hit up a few clubs tonight. Party like a rock star and check on some cute niggas and bitches. Who knows? You might get lucky and get you some dick."

"I hear you."

"Let's blow this spot., The clubs open early down here. They close early too, but there's a couple of after hour spots we can hit up. That's the only thing I hate about this city. And why I love going to New Orleans. Shit stay open late. You can buy alcohol every day and let your hair down. I can stay with you a couple of days and enjoy New Orleans. You know, keep you company while Keith's in jail."

"We'll see."

Her apartment was on the South West side of Houston just down the streets from Shape Town. They call it Hirthwood. The apartment was painted a raggedy blue and was in the fucking hood. Niggas were outside hustling dope and hoes were on the porch playing cards as loud music blasted. They were smoking weed and screaming and cursing their bad ass children who were running around playing. There was trash and stray dogs everywhere. I had told myself, if I ever made it out of the hood, I wouldn't ever come back. I meant it.

As I got out of the car, I looked around. "Bitch, this is where you stay."

"Bitch, it's hard times for me right now. Bitch, I strip for a living at different clubs, and sometimes I don't feel like doing that shit. I'm thirty-three and still shaking my ass in the club. Bitch, that's not a good look. But I can't get a good job because my fucking record is fucked up. Plus, I ain't trying to work for nobody the rest of my life."

"I hear you, bitch, When I get straight, I'm going to put you down. I got you."

"I hear you."

Her apartment was a small one-bedroom unit. "Brittney! This shit too small. Where am I going to sleep?"

"I know. I'm going to get us a room at the Holiday Inn. I'm not about to leave my Benz in the hood. My shit ain't never going to get stolen."

"I'll grab some clothes."

A little later we walked into a room with twin beds at a Holiday Inn. "Now, this is more like it," I said.

"I'm going to get into the shower."

"I'll be right behind you."

"You can join me if you want." She smiled back at me.

"Don't tempt me."

"Whatever. You faking." She closed the bathroom door.

While waiting, I unpacked a few things and checked my phone to see if I missed any messages. I hadn't.

A little later, Brittney emerged from the bathroom with a towel wrapped around here.

"It's all yours."

I jumped in the shower washing myself with strawberry body wash. I dried off and walked back into the room. Brittney was still getting dressed. I put on some strawberry Victoria's Secret lotion. I put on a white Victoria's Secret G-string with matching bra. I sprayed some Victoria's Secret perfume on me. I pulled on my tight red Gucci jeans that had my ass sitting right with a white Gucci button down blouse, I was wearing some black and red Gucci heals.

I didn't have to do anything with my hair since it was still cut short. That was why I did it, so I could just get up and go. I put on some eyeliner and lip gloss, and I was ready to go.

Brittney was wearing blue leggings with a white blouse and some white and blue red bottom heals.

"Bitch, let's hit the club," she said.

We pulled up to this club on the South West called Carros. The parking lot was packed with all kinds of cars, trucks and bikes sitting on chrome rims and with tinted windows.

"Damn. This motherfucker is packed out here. There's a long line wrapped around the corner!" I said.

"Yeah, it be this way every Friday night. Balling ass niggas be out here in Panameras, Audi R8, Mclarens and Bentleys. These motherfucking niggas getting money in Houston."

"The dope game must be nice to niggas."

"Bitch, these niggas out here ain't getting nothing less than fifty or better."

"Well, I ain't going to wait in line to get in a club."

"I got this."

"Bitch, Houston's changed a lot since I been out here."

"It sure have. It's built up out here, and the coke trade is plentiful."

"I see."

"Back in the day, J Prince was running everything down here."

"He still the man. He got his hand in everything still."

We got out the truck and walked straight to the front door. Brittney whispered something in the black, bald bouncer's ear, and he let us straight in. Another bouncer took us to the VIP section. A waitress brought us a couple of bottles of Peach Cîroc and a bucketful of ice. It was jam-packed in the club. I was talking wall to wall. The club was big with two bars, a large wooden dance floor and a big OJ booth on a small stage. Mirrors and red chairs lined the outside walls, and there were a lot of fine ass guys and women in here.

"You got a lot of pull in here," I said.

"Yeah, something like that. I know the nigga who own it. I used to push work for him back in the game."

As we were sipping on drinks, a tall, cute, brown-skinned, built brother walked up to us. He looked like Michael Jordan. He and Brittney hugged one another.

"Hey, Frank."

"They told me you were in the building. Long time, no see or hear. What's been happening with you?"

"Nothing. I've been chilling. I got out to show my best friend around. She in town for a week."

"Nice to meet you, pretty lady." He kissed my hand.

"Same here." I smiled.

"Everything good,"

"Yeah, but I need a few dollars."

He reached in his pocket, pulled out a knot, and gave it to her. "Call me. Drinks are on the house. Enjoy." He hugged both of us and walked off.

"Bitch, why ain't you fucking him?" I asked.

"Bitch, there's a rumor going around he got that pack."

"What AIDS?"

"Yeah, on top of that, that nigga is fucking every hoe in the city. He cool though. Weight made some money back in the game, but as for me fucking him. never. We just good friends. Plus, when I went to the Feds, I could have brought his ass down and couple of other niggas in the city. But I didn't, so when they see me, they give me my respect and throw me some bread every now and then. It's all love. Come on, I feel like shaking my ass."

"Me too. Must be the liquor."

We were drunk as hell, dancing on each other and on hoes and niggas too. We were sweating all over the place. We left the club at two in the morning. I don't know how we made it back to the hotel.

Caught Up in the Life

Walking through the door, I kicked off my shoes and got out of my clothes and fell in bed as drunk as hell. The next thing I knew Brittney was between my legs eating my pussy out. I was soaking wet.

I wanted to move her off me, but I needed some human contact. I hadn't been with Icy in over six months. So, I let her handle her business and grabbed her face, grinding my pussy in her mouth and face as she ate my pussy and asshole out. She licked and sucked on my clit, making me cum all in her mouth and face. I came so hard that I passed out on her.

I woke up the next morning with a headache. I heard the shower running as I found my purse and popped an Advil. I walked into the bathroom while Brittney was showering and took a piss. I felt so bad about falling asleep on her last night.

I pulled the shower curtain back and got in and began tongue kissing her. I moved down on her and began sucking and licking on her pussy. She grabbed my head. grinding her pussy in my faces as she came all in my mouth. I stood up and kissed her. We got out the shower, drying each other off.

"Now, that's how you make up for last night," she said.

"I figure I owed you that much."

"I'm going to holla at this nigga and see what's up."

"You need to take the money with you?"

"No, let me see what he's talking first."

I must had fell back asleep because my cell phone woke me up. I wasn't used to this going out shit. My body was letting me know it. I was hurting in spots I didn't know I had.

"Bitch, you coming to get me or what?" Brittney asked.

"What time is it?"

"Ten."

"Damn, I've been sleeping."

"When you going to come get me?"

"Where are you?"

"I'm at home."

"Why didn't you come back to the hotel?"

"I needed to make a couple of runs and get some more clothes."

"I'm getting up now."

I jumped in the shower to wash my ass. I put on a yellow lace thong and bra, and some yellow and pink legging. I put on my pink and yellow LV blouse with some white LV open toes heels. I got my white LV purse and jumped in the truck.

I pulled up to Brittney's apartment and blew the horn. She came out wearing some light blue tight Guess jeans, red button-down blouse and black red bottom heels. Her hair was cut short like mine but dyed blue.

"Bitch, it took you long enough!" she began

"Bitch! I fell back to asleep after you left. My body is not used to this shit. I haven't been out like this in years."

"I hear you."

"Where are we going?"

"To my favorite strip club on the North. Them hoes is butt naked. The Harlem Night. That's where it goes down at."

"Okay, what is dude talking about?"

"Eighteen. But he's waiting on a shipment. He told me to hit him up tomorrow."

We walked into the Harlem Night. I looked at all the bad ass, butt-naked bitches on the stage and on the floor giving lap dances to niggas and hoes. Hoes were coming up to Brittney, hugging and kissing her.

"Bitch, you know a lot of people in here."

"Yeah, that's because I strip in here from time to time."

"Oh."

We went to the bar and got a bottle of Patron and two thousand dollars in ones. We sat close to the stage watching different hoes perform as we did a shot of Tequila. One fine, black and Dominican bitch came out who looked like Nicki Minaj, body shape and all. I walked over and watched her bust it open as I threw up some ones.

After she finished, she came from the back to give me a lap dance. Brittney had a few hoes give her one too. We went to another strip club called Dreams. A lot of bad bitches were in there too. We threw a few ones and got drunk. Brittney bought some weed and we got fuck up.

I really don't know how we made it back to the hotel this time. All I know is I woke up the next evening with a hangover and that bad Dominican in bed with me. I pulled the cover back and looked at her big fine ass and face. The bitch was fine as hell with a big soft black ass. She was really cute, but I didn't remember fucking her.

As I got out of bed, I saw that Brittney had a bad yellow bone in bed with her. I went to the bathroom. While sitting on the toilet, I smiled as last night came back to me.

Back in the room, I saw Brittney talking on the phone and the other hoes were getting dressed.

The Dominican chick came over and kissed me. "I had a good time last night I'll call you."

"All right," I watched them both walk out the door.

"I'm going to go holla at him," Brittney said.

"Here the money. Be safe."

When she left, I went and grabbed me something to eat and went back to bed. I got up four hours later. I checked my phone, but Brittney hadn't called. I was starting to worry. I hope she hadn't got busted or run off with the fucking money.

As I was about to call, she came in carrying some McDonald's in her hand.

"Damn, what took you so long? I was getting worried. It's been over four hours."

"My bad. This dumb ass nigga Eric got working for him had me waiting for the fucking work to come."

"Well, you could have called me at least to let me know what was up. I was a nervous wreck in this bitch. I didn't know what to do. I didn't want you to go to jail behind me."

"Calm down. It's alright. I'm happy to see you still care about a bitch, but I'm good."

"You got it?"

"Here's the stuff," She handed me the McDonald's bag. It was wrapped up in plastic with tape around it. It smelled strong. I took it out of the bag and looked at it. The key of cocaine amazed me. I had never in my life seen this much cocaine at one time. I had seen crack rocks in the hood, but never a whole brick. The prosecutors said Keith was moving five thousand kilos at a time.

"How much?"

"Eighteen. Here's six back."

"Keep two."

"Thanks."

"Bitch, it been fun, but I got to hit the highway tonight."

We took a shower and got down for the last time before I hit the road. She helped me pack my stuff. We hugged and kissed. She helped me stash the coke. I pulled off nervous hell as I hit the Interstate, I didn't play on the radio or talk on the phone. I was focused on the task at hand and was trying to get back to the city with this key of coke.

I got to be out my damn mind. Trying to be a drug dealer. If Keith ever finds out about this shit, he's going to kill me.

Finally, I made it back to New Orleans, I breathed easier. I called the prosecutor.

"I got a connect," I told him.

"It's time to be a player. Make that money."

I hung up and called my mother to check on the kids. "How's everything with the kids?"

"It's all good."

"I'm back."

"Okay."

"Love you. Bye."

I went to my bedroom and pulled out the key of coke. I still couldn't believe it. I put it in the top of my closet making sure my kids couldn't reach it. I wondered how I was going to get off all this shit.

The things a bitch go through for her husband. I guess a bitch will do *anything* for her husband.

Chapter 16

Shantell

I pulled up to Jackie's house and grabbed the bag from under my seat. I walked fast up to her front door and knocked.

I had popped awake at two in the morning when she came into my head. She used to sell weed and coke for her ex-boyfriend in the strip club. She knew motherfuckers who bought cocaine.

When she opened the door, I went straight to her kitchen.

"Bitch, what's so important that you had to come to my house at three in the morning. I could have been getting some."

"Bitch, I need your help getting of this." I pulled the key from my bag and set it on the table.

"Bitch, where you get that from?"

"Don't worry about all that. Can you help me get off it?"

"Yeah, but we going to have to break it down."

"Whatever that means. I'm green when it comes to selling drugs. It's not my forte."

"Well, I'll give you the game, but afterwards you got to tell me where you got it from."

"My friend Brittney helped me get it. I need to make some money because I'm on hard times. You know they took everything from me."

"I got you."

"Look, I don't want to meet nobody. You can handle that. All I need for you to do is bring me my money back. I'll look out for you."

"So, you my pimp now?"

"Don't play, you down or what?"

"I'm down. This could be my ticket to opening my shop."

"No, bitch, I'm going to show you how it's done, and you're going to put in work too." I know I should tell her what's going on, but I don't need her all up in my business. People tend to act funny when you ask them to help you sell drugs to set people up. I just wanted to pop her off and help her get her shop. We could help each other. She got what she wanted, I got what I wanted. Fair exchange was no robbery.

She came back to the kitchen carrying a scale.

"What's that?"

"This is a triple beam. It measures the weight of the dope. Get those sandwich bags out of cabinet. I learned a lot from my ex-boyfriend who used to sell coke in the hood. He taught me to break them down.

We sat at the table for hours smoking weed as we weighed and bagged that shit up. A lot of shit went into being a drug dealer. I saw that now.

"This is how they sell it in the clubs?" I asked.

"Twenty, and fifty-dollar bags. Damn, Keith never showed the game to you?"

"No, bitch, I never saw that side of Keith. He kept all that stuff away from me. The Feds said he was selling keys all over the city."

"Damn. That nigga was on a whole other level. Look, ounces is twenty-eight grams. There are thirty-six ounces in a kilo. You're supposed to cut this shit and make a lot of money, but I like it raw."

"Bitch, you snort this shit?"

"Yeah, bitch, that's how I know it's good coke. The girls do it all the time at the club to stay awake or to block their trick out. I do it because I like to get high, and I like the nut I get from it. My pussy gets soaking wet. It's the best sexual nut I ever have. I don't even have to have sex with a nigga. I snort this powder and my pussy be cuming like a motherfucker."

"I hear you."

"Bitch, you never tried it in college."

"No, I did some wild shit, but snorting coke wasn't one."

"You want to try some now? I tell you, bitch, it's going to have you so wet, and your pussy is going to be cuming like a motherfucker."

"Well, I need to see you hit a line first."

She dug a pink fingernail into the powder, then raised it to her nose, snorting it. "Fuck! This some good shit. This shit is pure." She leaned back. "You try it. My pussy got soaking wet that fast."

"Hell no."

"Suppose I ain't with you, and you got to score? What are you going to do? Some motherfucker will sell you bad shit. You need to know."

I thought about her point. And suppose a nigga wanted me to snort a line to prove I'm not the police. "Okay, let me hit this shit. You made a point."

She dug her nail back in the coke and raised it to my nose. I hesitated for a second, but then snorted it off her nail. I felt funny at first like I was floating. Then my pussy started getting wetter and wetter like I was cuming on myself. I leaned back in the chair enjoying the feeling.

"How do you feel?" Jackie asked.

"God... like I'm flowing... on cloud nine."

"Oh, shit. "

"What?"

"Your nose is bleeding."

"What? My nose bleeding ?" I started to freak out.

"It's all right. Just hold your head back." She pressed a towel to my face.

"It's because it your first time. The coke is pure. It'll pass."

"Bitch, my nose is burning."

"Just give it a second. It'll pass. I promise."

"Okay." A few minutes later everything was good again.

"Now how do you feel? You want to try some more?"

"Yeah, just one more time."

We finish weighing and bagging the coke high as a motherfucker. We sat spaced out in her kitchen. When I left, the sun was coming up.

"I'll call you when I sell this stuff tonight."

"Thanks."

I left her with four ounces to sell and took the rest with me. With my high coming down, I fell into bed and went straight to sleep.

I woke up to the phone ringing. The clock said it was six in the evening. It was Keith.

"Hey, baby!" I answered,

"Where you been? I've been calling all day."

"Sorry. I've been running today. Trying to get my business straight at the shop."

"Okay. I got your pictures."

"You like them?"

"You know I do."

"Thought you would."

"Don't come this weekend. Some nigga got stabbed. We going to be on lock down for a couple months."

"Okay,"

"I've got to go. I'll hit you up later. I love you."

"Love you back. Be safe in there."

"You already know."

When we hung up, I lay back down for a few hours. I got up about midnight and fixed a bite to eat. I went and soaked in a hot bubble bath. I was thinking of how my life had changed in the last four years. I went from having it all to having to struggle to pay my bills. Now I was selling coke for the people who fucked up my life in the first place. Life was crazy.

As I got out the tub Jackie called. "I need you to bring me some more stuff. I need three more ounces. This shit is booming out chere."

"Damn, that shit went quick."

"Yeah, these hoes and niggas loving it in chere. They got a party going on up her."

"I'll be there in thirty minutes."

"I'll be waiting for you outside."

I threw on some jogging pants, a sweatshirt and some white Air Max tennis shoes. I grabbed the stuff out the closet and stuffed it in my purse.

When I got to the club, Jackie was out front waiting on me. She jumped in and handed me four stacks. I pulled the ounces out of my purse.

"Bitch, it's booming in chere. I might need you to come back with more."

"Just call me."

She got out the car, and I drove off. I couldn't believe how quick that shit sold.

Jackie hit me a few more times. I had to make a couple more runs to the club after that.

Chapter 17

Shantell

Jackie and I counted the money she had made the night before. It was eighteen thousand dollars.

"Bitch, we made eighteen thousand in a matter of hours," I said.

"I told your ass it was booming."

"That's crazy."

"That's why niggas be addicted to fast money."

"I see now. Bitch, here's two grand for helping me."

"It's all good. I told you I got you."

We finished bagging the other half of the brick." "Bitch, I got to go home and get some sleep. I got to go shake my ass tonight."

She grabbed four ounces. "Okay, you be safe."

"Always," she said as she pulled a gun from her bag.

"Let me see that. It looks like the one I got."

"Yeah, it's a black 38."

"I feel you."

"I need this for those crazy motherfuckers at the club. They be trying to stalk a bitch and shit after the club."

"That's what up."

"Later."

I walked into my bedroom and put the money in Keith's small safe. That was one thing the Feds didn't take. He kept fifty thousand in it with our passports. I was going to fill it back up. The Feds said I had to set this motherfucker up, but they didn't tell me to give them any money.

That evening! I walked into the strip club in the French Quarter on Bourbon Street. I was nervous as hell. The club was called V LIVE and I had five ounces of coke in my purse. There were a lot of undercover police in the Quarter.

I looked around for Jackie's ass. Black and white bitches were walking around butt-naked, giving lap dances and dancing on the stage. Jackie came from the back butt-naked with her ass shaking and a money clip full of ones. She had on six-inch heels. Her face was made up and her red and blue weave hung down to her ass. She looked totally different.

"Hey girl... here's some money. You bought more stuff?"

We went to the bathroom. I gave her two ounces and kept the three. I sat in the club hustling with Jackie. I had said I wouldn't do that. When she went on stage, she sent a couple girls I knew from high school to buy from me. I went to the bathroom to sell to them.

Later, Jackie come front the back, dressed. We left there and hit a few more clubs. Jackie knew some people that liked to buy coke. The money was coming so fast. I didn't know this many motherfuckers liked coke.

We posted up at this bar called Decatur. People were coming left and right buying three and four bags at a time. We stayed in the Quarter all night selling drugs. I saw why my husband didn't make it home some nights. The money would be coming so fast you didn't want to leave.

We stayed until the sun came up, partying and shit.

***

Three weeks later

I still had about had five ounces of coke left. This shit with Jackie was cool, but I needed to start moving weight if I wanted to get to my husband's level and meet his connect. I needed to find people that wanted to buy ounces, four half, nine ounces, half keys and keys. Not this nickel and dime shit. It wasn't going to get it.

I needed to find somebody in the hood and take that shit over. I rented *Deep Cover* to see how Larry Fishburne did it. He shot a motherfucker and got his respect from the streets. He moved in taking the guy's blocks, pushing coke until he was big enough to meet the cartel. I already had Brittney as my plug for the keys. I just needed to find someone who would move coke as fast as I could get it.

As I drove down M.L.K. near Myoid Projects and the Melphomene Projects, I spotted Kesha's fat ass crossing the street. It hit me. She was the one I needed to see. This was one hustling bitch. She could move anything and knew the whole city, including people in the right places.

Kesha and I used to be best friends, but we grew apart when I moved out. I blew my horn to get her attention as she was about to go in the project store.

She looked at my car as she tried to figure out who it was riding in a Bentley trying to stop her.

"Kesha, bitch! Come over her with your fat ass," I said, after rolling down the window.

"Shantell, bitch! Hey!" She walked over the car. "I don't know who you was pulling up on me in a Bentley in the fucking hood. I see life's been treating you good, huh?"

"If you only knew."

"You doing better than me, bitch. I'm out chere struggling. Niggas ain't trying to give a bitch shit out chere. I need to make some money."

"I might have something for you."

"Bitch, let talk." She got in my car.

Kesha was a chubby, high yellow chick and ghetto Fabulous. She looked like Monique the comedian. You couldn't tell her she wasn't sexy. She even stripped a couple of times. Her confidence was through the roof. She fell like she could get any nigga she wanted too. And believe it or not, the bitch was fucking niggas that looked like they were straight out of G.Q. Most of them were straight out of prison.

She had two kids, a boy and a girl. They looked just like her. Her baby daddy got killed in a shoot-out with the police. To show how sexy this bitch thought she was. She was wearing some shorts that were riding up her ass with a pink wife beater with some white LV loafers. She had long blue track hanging down her back.

"So, what we talking?" she asked

"You want to move some ounces of coke for me?"

"Hell, yeah where that shit at? I need some money."

I turned into the projects. This shit looked so different from when I used to stay back here. After Katrina they went to tearing shit down. They tore down almost all the projects in the city, but there were still a few parts where niggas still tried to hustle dope.

As I pulled up to her apartment, I noticed my side of the projects was torn down. I saw a few niggas hustling in the breezeway. Trash was everywhere. Kids and dogs were running around all over. Bitches were sitting on their porches smoking weed and talking loud with their music blasting from their houses. They had repainted the projects' bricks black and tan.

"You think you can move it back here?"

"Hell, they got a few niggas moving work here, but nothing major. There's one nigga who thinks he's running shit back chere, but he ain't working with shit. For the most part, they got niggas coming back here from all over trying to sell and get work. But ain't nobody major back here. This little nigga name Fire back here playing with a few keys, but the nigga get blowed off heroin. One day, he's on. The next day, he's falling off. But they ain't got nobody back here moving a lot of weight. You can take this shit over back here if you got weight. There ain't a lot of people in the city moving coke. A lot of people is moving over to heroin, because coke prices went up."

Her apartment was all laid out and not fucked up like a lot of hoes shit in the projects. She had a big, white leather sofa, matching white carpet and a big flat screen hanging on the wall in the living room. Her kitchen had a big glass table with the matching chairs. There weren't roaches or rats running around her apartment. We sat at the table in the kitchen.

"Bitch, you got some weed?" I asked.

"Bitch, you smoke weed now?"

"Bitch, I turned into a weed head the last couple of years. Lucky a bitch ain't smoking crack. The fucking way I've been stressed the fuck out about my husband going to Federal prison for thirty years."

"Damn, bitch. He must have really been large in the streets."

She came back to the kitchen and handed me a lit blunt. I hit the weed and started choking, "Damn, this is some good shit."

"Yeah, this is Kush from Cali. Fifty dollars a gram. What did your man get thirty for?"

"Bitch ass nigga, Dave Green, ratted on him over some back in the day shit. And the Feds bought him into it. The nigga dead now. Somebody killed his ass at the halfway not too long ago."

"That's how them soft ass niggas do now days. Who's your husband?"

"Keith Washington."

"You're talking about cute Keith that had all the work in the city and was fucking all the hoes?"

"That's him."

"I know Keith. He used to give bricks to this nigga out the Magnolia I was fucking with."

"Where are your kids?"

"My mother got custody. I lost them when I went to jail for check fraud. I did a year and a half in the Feds. So, my mother got them until I get off probation."

"Are you sure you want to move this work?"

"Bitch, I'm broke. I get a welfare check for five hundred dollar a month and food stamps. I still got to take care of my kids. My mother don't do shit for free. I'm going to move the work."

"I'll bring you five ounces, and we'll go from there. I'll be back in a couple of hours."

"I'll be here."

We talked a little longer.

"I got to go. I'll hit you up when I'm on my way back."

"Bitch, you need to bring that shit ASAP. It's about to be Christmas, and my kids want all the latest phones and pads."

"I got you."

We hugged each other. I got in my car and drove off.

***

Later that night, I was back in Kesha's apartment, smoking weed and watching her cook up the nine ounces I had brought her. She took out baking soda and test tubes. She added the last ounces of coke with some baking soda and water. She put it on the stove and started mixing it. I had never seen cocaine cooked up before.

"Why you're cooking it?"

"That's what they be running for back chere. Heroin and crack. Powder sell okay, but not like this crack."

117

"Oh."

As she finished, it was in a big ball. She dropped it on the table. I picked it up to look at it.

"Damn, that shit is hard," I said.

"I whip it."

"What you mean?"

"I made it into more than nine ounces. It's like twelve ounces."

"You can do that?"

"Bitch, I been fucking the best dope boys in the world, and they show me everything in the game."

"I see."

"We going to get this money."

I watched her cut the ball down to fifty and hundred dollar slabs. She also cut out small rocks off it. We went out to her porch at about midnight. She put the word out that she had big rocks and gave some to junkies to try. Motherfuckers started coming back to back, spending twenty or a hundred dollars. For the most part, she was selling fifty and hundred dollar slabs, and it was booming

In less than two hours, she sold half of the twelve ounces she made. We counted the money. It was every bit of six hundred thousand dollars, and the junkies kept knocking on her door all night.

"Bitch, this going to be all night," she said.

"Damn, you really rolling."

"I told you."

"Here's two grand. Sell the rest and hit me up when you finish."

"All right."

I jumped in my car. I got somebody I could rock with. I was in the game now. All I had to do was start buying bricks.

Chapter 18

Shantell

Three days later, Jackie and I headed west on 1-10 for Houston. Brittney was expecting us. Jackie wanted to come because she had never been to Houston. She spent Katrina in Atlanta. I didn't mind bringing her along because I needed someone to ride back with me after scoring the work. It would keep me from being all nervous, and I would have someone to talk to.

Kesha got off all the work for me. She still had a few ounces of her own that would hold her over until I got back. I made forty grand off that one brick. That bitch Kesha was a hustling motherfucker. Hard work and hunger was what my team needed. That was the only way I would ever get this connect.

Jackie and Brittney should get along. Those hoes had a lot of shit in common. They both stripped, and they both liked hoes. The only difference was that I never got down with Jackie. Not that I'd say no. I just never pursued it. Since I made forty five grand, I was going to try to cop two and half this time.

As we neared Houston, I called Brittney.

"What's up, bitch? Where you at?"

"I'm coming in downtown."

"Meet me on the Southside. I moved into a better apartment."

"No, meet me at the Best Western."

"I'm on my way."

I got a room with twin beds. We rested for an hour before Brittney carne.

"What's up, bitch?" I said, as we hugged.

"Nothing." She hugged me back and came in the room. She had on some short ass blue jeans shorts with her ass hanging out and a pink T-shirt tied at the side. She wasn't wearing a bra. She had on some white Air Max. Her hair was still short but green this time.

"Why the hoochie dressing?" I asked.

"Bitch, it's hot in Texas in the summer. I just threw this on. Bitch, I don't have on draws either. A bitch's pussy got to breathe.

"I feel you."

She turned to Jackie, "Hey, I'm Brittney."

"Girl, give me a hug," Jackie said. "I've heard so much about you. College friend, right?"

"Yea, that's me. I'm glad to meet you. A friend of Shantell is a friend of mine. I need to call the plug. To see what's good."

"I need two and a half," I said.

"I see you moving up in the world."

"I thought we would go out and have a good time with Jackie. She's never been here before."

"Okay, we'll have a blast." She turned to Jackie, "You like strip clubs?"

"Bitch, I'm a stripper," Jackie said.

"Me too. That's what's up." They said slapping each other five.

Brittney called the plug.

"What's good," he answered.

"Two and a half."

"Tomorrow."

"Okay." She hung up.

"What did he say?" I asked

"Tomorrow."

"That's cool. We can hit the mall and get some clothes, so we can go out."

"You're treating because my ass is broke," Brittney said.

"I got you."

***

We went to Shape Town mall. I treated them to an outfit and some shoes, so we could go out that night.

That was the least I could do for all the work they had done. We sat in the food court talking shit about fine ass niggas and hoes walking by. We debated who we would fuck and who we wouldn't.

I got up to throw the trash away. A handsome, fine brown-skinned brother walked up to me. He looked like a young Denzel Washington. His hair was cut short with waves going through it. He was tall, about six feet and ripped up like he was an athlete. He wore a tight, black shirt and some blue jeans that were fitting him right. I got a glimpse of what he was packing because his jeans were snug down there. He was wearing big, black gator boots. The brother had some big feet. You know what they say about big feet.

"Excuse me, I couldn't help but see how beautiful you are. I had to come over to give a compliment and see if I could give you a good time."

The brother's teeth were snow white and beautiful. This brother was fine. He looked as if he had just stepped out of GQ.

"Thank you for the compliment." I smiled at the brother.

"My name is Darrell," He held out a well-manicured hand.

"Nice to meet you. My name is Winda Smith," I lied as I shook his hand.

"The pleasure's all mine." He kissed my hand.

My pussy instantly got wet. The brother had my undivided attention.

"You never answered my question," he said.

"Which was?"

"Can I take you out sometime?"

"Well, I'm from out of town chilling with my friends. Right now is not good."

"I see. Here's my number if you change your mind. Please, give me a call."

He kissed my hand.

I smiled. "Will do."

I put his number in my pocket and walked away, putting a little more twist in my walk. Something told me to look back. Sure enough, he was looking at my ass. I smiled at Jackie and Brittney who stared at the brother with their mouth open.

"Damn, you bitches close your mouths and stop drooling."

"Bitch, who is that fine brother you were talking to? He was staring at your ass. I'd like to drink his tub water," Brittney said.

"He want to take me out."

"And what did you say? Jackie asked.

"I told him I'm from out of town, and I'm here with my girlfriends, so I have to pass."

"Bitch, you stupid. I would have went out with him and fucked on the first date. That brother would have been my baby daddy," Brittney said.

"I keep telling her ass she needs to get out and have fun. Date other motherfuckers and get her some dick. Fuck Keith. Life goes on. That nigga' s been gone four years now. You think he'd be waiting to get him some pussy if you had thirty years in prison?" Jackie said.

"Bitch, you got his number?" Brittney asked.

"Yes."

"You need to be calling his fine ass. See if you can suck and lick on his dick. And see how well he eats pussy. Ride his dick until the sun comes up." Brittney tried to counsel me.

"For real," Jackie agreed.

"Whatever. Let's go." I ended the conversation, and later we pulled up to this club called Maxwell's on the SouthSide. It was for the grown and sexy. You had to be over thirty to get in.

This was where the real ballers came to have a good time. There were lawyers, doctors, business owners, brothers and sisters who were making real moves in the streets. It was a mixed crowd of black, white, Spanish, and Asian people. Everybody that was anybody in the hip hop world also came here to party. There were all kinds of foreign cars and trucks in the lot.

We stepped out of my Bentley looking like some boss bitches. I had on a red Donna Karen dress with matching open-toe heels. I was carrying a small white handbag from Donna Karen. I was wearing a couple of pieces of Dior jewelry. Brittney had on a little, black Gucci dress with high heel Gucci sandals. Jackie was wearing a light blue Prada dress with light blue open-toe stiletto boots.

The line was wrapped around the corner. I tipped the bouncer a hundred dollars and he let us in the club. We went straight the VIP room and ordered bottles of Peach Cîroc. The club had two floors. One was for hip hop, and the other was for slow R&B music. There were two DJs on each floor along with two bars. Two wooden dance floors were jam packed with bad bitches and fine brothers.

Caught Up in the Life

"Come on ya'll. Let's go on the dance floor. I don't want to be in here like a fishbowl," Brittney said.

I agreed. "We came here to party and let our hair hang down. We might find some hot piece," Jackie added.

As we went to the dance floor, I felt someone grab my hand. I looked around, and it was Darrell. He was looking right in his white linen outfit. He walked up to me, and I felt butterflies in my stomach.

"I didn't know you come out here," he said.

"I usually don't, but my girls took me out."

"Where are they?"

"Over there."

Jackie and Brittney were shaking their asses on some niggas. He whispered something to me, and I followed him upstairs where the DJ was playing some old school R&B: "Nobody" by Keith Sweat and Kut Close was on.

"Come on, let's dance," Darrell suggested.

At first, I hesitated, but then I thought, what the hell. I hadn't been touch by a man in a long time.

He led me onto the dance floor. He held me around my waist just right. Not too tight. I held him around his neck. Thank God for heels. We slow danced. His Polo Blue cologne smelled so good that it was driving me crazy. It was the same kind Keith wore. My pussy was so wet I thought I was about to cum on myself on the dance floor.

He whispered in my ear with his Barry White voice, which made me even wetter, "I'm not holding you too tight, am I?"

"No," I smiled at him.

"You feel soft, and you smell so good. You look beautiful tonight."

I felt cum dripping in my panties and running down my leg. Lord this man was turning me on.

"Do you want to get out of here and go somewhere?" he asked. I thought for a second and decided, fuck it. I hadn't been on a date in a while, and the brother was so hot and sexy.

"Yeah, but I need to stop by the ladies' room first."

"I'll be waiting at the bar."

I walked in the bathroom and checked the stalls. I pulled off my thong, washed it in the sink, and stuffed it in my purse. I used some wipes to clean my pussy off. I sprayed perfume on me and checked myself in the mirror before I walked out. You never know. The brother might want to go down on me. I didn't want to smell like pussy.

I found Darrell at the bar. "I'm ready. I just need to tell my friends I'm leaving with you."

We walked downstairs looking for them. I found them in the VIP room talking to some niggas and hoes. I left Darrell and went over to Jackie and Brittney.

"Bitch, where you been?" Brittney asked.

"I'm about to leave."

"With who?" Jackie said.

"Darrell. The guy I met at the mall."

They looked at him at the bar. "Damn, that nigga is fine," Brittney said." See if he has a brother."

"Here's the keys. I'll call later."

"Get some for me," Brittney said.

"About fucking time," added Jackie.

We left the club and went to a Benihana restaurant. We were eating steak and potatoes and drinking red wine.

"Where are you from?" he asked.

"Florida."

"Which part?"

"M.I.A. "

"I've heard it's booming down there. I've never been."

"I might take you one day."

"For sure."

Darrell seemed like a nice man. I hated lying to him, but I didn't need him all up in my business, especially since I was working for the Feds. I didn't need him trying to find me on Facebook. I would probably never talk to him after tonight. I just didn't have time to get my feelings caught up with a man. I had enough shit to worry about.

I decided that I would fuck him, then forget him.

"Where are you from?" I asked

"I'm from here."

"As handsome as you are, why aren't you married or have a girlfriend?"

"I was married for ten years. She died from cancer."

"Sorry to hear that."

"I've learned to live with it. What about you?"

"Single. Never married."

"You want to get out of here."

The next thing I knew we were back in his condo getting naked and kissing. He lay me on his king-sized bed and removed my bra. He started at my toes, sucking them one by one. I just moaned in pleasure. He moved up slowly, kissing the inside of my thighs.

He slid his tongue up to my stomach, kissing on my navel. He moved up to my breasts sucking on one nipple while caressing the other. He moved back down to my pussy and spread my legs. He licked my clit as I grinded my pussy in his face. "Yeah, right there. Don't stop.... I'm cuming."

He sucked on my pussy lips and clit until I started to shake, cuming into his mouth. As I was cuming back to back, he eased his rock hard dick inside of me and put my legs over his shoulders driving deep inside my pussy walls. That shit felt like he was deep in my stomach. As he thrusted in and out of me, my body tensed up. I began cuming back to back. I dug my nails in his back. He flipped me over on my stomach, climbed on top me and began to slow grind his dick in my pussy.

I grabbed his hands as our bodies tightened as we came together as one. I felt his hot nut shoot all in my pussy. It felt so good, I came harder. I lay my head on his chest and fell asleep.

I got up the next morning before the sun came up. I looked at him sleeping while I grabbed my things, called a cab and left. I felt guilty but pleased at the same time. My body needed it. I could not to lie. A bitch felt a whole lot better, but I felt guilty because I had never cheated on my husband. I kept telling myself there was nothing wrong with a one night stand. Men did it all the time.

Back at the hotel, those two hoes were sleeping in bed together, butt naked. I knew they would get it on. Those hoes were one and the same. I pulled off the covers to fuck with them. "You bitches need to get up."

"Get the fuck out," Brittney said putting the covers back over her head. I grabbed some clothes from my suitcase and took a hot shower, letting the water flow over my body. I was still smiling about last night. My body felt rejuvenated and stress free. I hadn't cum like that in years. There was nothing like some good dick to get a bitch's mind right.

Back in the room, Brittney and Jackie were checking their phones. They looked me over. I didn't realize I was whistling with a big smile on my face.

"A bitch must have got her some dick last night," Jackie said.

"Bitch, you need to stay out my business." I tried to hold back a laugh.

"Bitch, you lying." Brittney came over and took the shirt out of my hand.

"Bitch, give me back my shirt."

"No, bitch. Tell us what happened first," Jackie said.

"And don't leave out any details," Brittney said.

"There's nothing to tell. We went to a restaurant, had a couple of drinks, ate, and talked. I fell asleep on his couch. I got up this morning and caught a cab here. "

"And you expect us to believe that shit. We've been your best friends your whole life. We know when your punk ass is lying." Brittney said.

"Now, spill the fucking Tee," Jackie added

"Ain't nothing that'll have you whistling this time of morning but some good dick," Brittney said.

"Did you suck him good? What about him eating the pussy?" Jackie insisted.

"No, bitch, I did not suck his dick, but he did eat my pussy."

"Bitch, I knew it." said Jackie.

"Tell it all." Brittney said.

"Bitches, the dick was good as a motherfucker. The dick ten inches and had me climbing the walls. Bitch, my toes curled, and it felt like he was about to burst through me. Bitches, I came like never before." I joined in with them, laughing.

"I've been telling you to get some dick for the longest," Jackie told me.

126

"So, how do you feel?" Brittney asked.

"Pleased but guilty at the same time."

"Guilty for what, bitch?" Jackie said" You got some dick."

"Bitch, for cheating on my husband."

'Bitch, fuck all that. The only ones going to know is us, God, and that big dick man. Fuck that guilty shit. If the shoe was on the other foot, Keith would be out here fucking everything with legs."

"You're right." I turned to Brittney. "Did Eric hit you back?"

"He said two o'clock."

"Okay,"

"Are you going to see him again?" Jackie asked.

"Who?"

"Bitch, the dick man."

"Hell, no. It was a one night stand."

"Whatever."

"Well since it was a one time thing, can I have his number?" Brittney asked.

"No," I smiled and walked back to the bathroom.

"Why not? You said you're not going to see him no more."

As I finished getting dressed, I was thinking about Darrell.

***

I left Jackie sleeping in the hotel, and Brittney left with the money to get the work. I decided to go to the mall and do some shopping for me and the kids. I missed their bad asses. I hadn't talked to them since they'd been at summer camp.

As I strolled into the mall, my phone rang. My heart skipped a beat. It was Darrell. I didn't want to answer, but he could just be checking on me. The brother did have some good dick, so he deserved for me to tell him I was okay. After all, I left without a word.

I nervously answered the phone.

"Hey, beautiful," he said. I was calling to see if you were all right. You left without saying anything."

"I'm all right. You were sleeping so good, I didn't want to wake you. My girl was worried about me."

"I'm glad to hear you're okay. Maybe, we can catch a movie tonight or something?"

"Not tonight. I'll be leaving Houston shortly. I'm going to spend my last day with my girls."

"When can I see you again?" Do you know when you'll come back to Houston?"

"I'm not sure, but I'll call you."

"I hope you call soon. I had a nice time with you."

"Me too. I'll call the next time I'm in town."

As I hung up, Brittney called. "Where you at?"

"The mall," I said.

"Meet me back at the hotel."

I made my way back to the hotel. Brittney helped me stash the two and a half keys in my car. We all hugged and kissed. Jackie and I headed back to New Orleans. It was raining on the way home, which was a good thing. The state troopers don't like stopping people in the rain. We made it back to New Orleans in about four and half hours.

Jackie and I broke one of the kilos down and snorted a bit to see if it was as good as before. I checked my messages. Darrell had been calling since I left Houston, but I wasn't planning on returning his calls. Keith had called a couple of times, but I didn't answer on the highway. I was focused on getting that shit back. Kesha called to tell me that she was out. I thought about calling her back but waited until Jackie and I were finished.

"I'm taking five ounces with me," Jackie said.

"Okay, be safe. Hit me up when you finish them."

After Jackie left I called my mother. "Hey, mom, you heard from the kids?"

"Yeah, they little bad asses called me and said they staying a couple more weeks."

"I'm back in the city. You need anything?"

"I need to get my hair and nails done."

"We'll go tomorrow."

"Please. I got a hot young piece I'm going on a date with."

"Call me tomorrow."

I hung up, grabbed nine ounces and called Kesha.

"I hope your ass is on the way."

"I'll be there in twenty."

"Good."

I pulled into the projects. Kesha was waiting on her porch. I got out of my car with a black LV bag over my shoulder and went inside. I put the nine ounces on the table. She lit a blunt and went to work.

After she finished, we sat on the porch smoking weed and selling crack. A young, black guy with dreads and tattoos on his face came up. He was wearing some skinny black jeans and a white wife beater. He looked like Lil' Duval. I just looked at him.

"Kesha, you know you in violation."

"Boy, what the fuck you talking about?"

"You taking my sells. That's what."

"Boy, you better get out my face. You don't run shit back chere."

"Kesha, you know how I get down."

"What? I'm supposed to be scared?"

"Stop short stopping my shit."

"Boy, whatever."

"I'm just going to tell you once."

"Whatever. Boy, you better move around."

"Girl, I'm out," I said. I was thinking as I drove off that this nigga was going to be a problem. I saw it already. He was going to have to go. Like Larry Fishburne did to the guy in *Deep Cover*.

Robert Baptiste

Chapter 19

Shantell

I looked for my husband in the visitation room with my pussy full of heroin. I know I said I wouldn't do it again, but this was how Keith was making his moves in prison. Even though I was keeping his books straight, I wanted him to be as comfortable as possible. So, I smuggled in dope every now and then to keep him happy. Until I could get him out, what else could I do?

He came up. We hugged and kissed as always. I slid off to the bathroom and left the heroin in the trash like before. When I walked out, he had moved.

"Why did you move way over here?"

"It's a blind spot. The camera can't see you."

I was wearing a sun dress with no pants. He began rubbing between my legs. He moved up toward my pussy and slid a finger in it. I became soaking wet as he played in it. He pulled his finger out, sucking the juice off it.

"Damn, you taste so good. I forgot how good your pussy tastes."

"You so nasty."

"Jerk me off."

"Boy, we going to get caught."

"No, we not. It's all good." He pulled his rock hard dick out.

I began to stroke him, nervously looking around to see if anyone was watching us. I played with his balls. His chest began to rise, and he started to breathe hard. He started to shake, cuming all over my hand.

I went back to the bathroom to wash my hands. The things a bitch would do for her husband. I came back wearing a big smile.

"Thanks for helping me relieve some stress," he kissed me.

Just then, guilt hit me. I thought about cheating on him with Darrell. I wanted to cry but held back my tears.

The C.O. announced that visitation was over. I was kind of glad because I was feeling so bad, I was about to tell on myself.

"Are you coming back next week?"

"I'll try, but the kids are coming back from camp."

"Okay, I love you."

"Love you back. Be safe in here."

"Always."

We hugged and kissed.

In my car, the guilt washed over me. I cried over cheating on my husband. I wanted my old life back because none of this shit would be happening. I was out here in the streets lying about selling dope for the Feds. I was keeping secret from my husband about my activities and fucking. On top of all that. I was working with the motherfuckers who put him in prison. I didn't sign up for this. I didn't want my marriage to be based on fucking lies.

"Damn! My life is real fucked up right now," I said to myself.

***

FOUR MONTHS LATER

Jackie and I were counting the money that she and Kesha had made. I had already made a couple more trip to Houston. Now I was playing with five bricks, and the shit was moving fast. I ran through three of them as fast as I got back to city. Kesha and Jackie knew people buying ounces and four and half at a time. Three bricks went fast when you were moving weight.

I called Brittney, "I'm coming down. I need eight chicken wings when I get there. "

"I got you." That was our code we used when It was time to score.

"Look, I'm about to go re-up. Take this key and move it. I'll give the other half to Kesha," I told Jackie.

I quickly packed my Gucci bag and stuffed the half key into it. I headed for Kesha's projects. I gave her the bag, and she gave me the money.

"I'm going to make a move. I'll be back in a couple of days. That should hold you over 'til I get back."

"I got a few people trying to get 9 ounces and half-bricks."

"We'll see what's up when I get back."

"Be safe."

At home, I packed a small bag. I wasn't going to be in Houston for more than two days. I sat in the room watching TV as I waited for Brittney. She had been gone for two hours. I was getting worried. It didn't take this long normally. About the time I was most nervous, she came in.

"Sorry it took so long. I was waiting on one of the runners to bring me the shit."

She opened the bag to show me eight bricks.

"That's what's up. Here's three grand."

"Thanks, bitch. you moving them bricks pretty fast, huh?"

"When the shit is good, you know how it goes. Be back in a couple of weeks."

"I'll be here. Be safe on the highway."

"I'll call when I make it back."

I was nervous as hell hitting 1-10 with a bag full of dope. What if I got busted? What about my kids? What if Keith found out? I was so happy to see Kenner Airport I didn't know what to do. My pussy and armpits were sweating out of control.

I dropped a couple bricks off with Jackie and a couple more with Kesha and got the money they'd made. I made a stash spot at my beauty supply store. I kept the dope and money in the safe in my office. I took two of the bricks home and broke one of them down like Jackie had showed me.

I sat at my house waiting for people to hit me up. It was another thing I said I wouldn't do. But when you're trying to climb the ladder, the workers can't be the only ones moving the work. So, Kesha and Jackie introduced me to a few people looking to buy large amounts.

I was in bed when the phone rang. It was Barry. Had been buying ounces.

"What's good?"

"I need a four way."

"Where you want to meet?"

"The apartments down the street from the Magnolia."

"Be there in thirty."

I pulled up to some torn down apartment down the street from the Magnolia. This was where all the niggas and hoes be hanging since they tore down the projects. They hustled everything back here from coke, dope, weed, and pills. I really didn't like corning back here because motherfucker got killed back here every day. Barry ran out of the hallway and got in my car. He was a cute red skinned boy with blue eyes and wavy hair. He favored Terrence Howard. He tried to hit on me every time I served him, but he was way too young for me. I'm too old to be playing games running behind some young boy who'd get me dick whipped. Plus, he was in the drug game. I didn't need any more stress with that.

He was one of Kesha's people. I gave him his half bricks. "What's good?" he asked

"Nothing. I need to get out these raggedy ass apartments. You know I don't like coming back here."

"You safe with me. When you gonna let me take you out?"

"Boy, I done told you. You're too young for me. Now, give me my money."

"I'll have you climbing the walls."

"I know, but you ain't going to get none of this. Get out my car."

"And you need to stop acting bad with me."

"Bye, boy. I got to make some more runs."

I stopped in the Calliope and served Blaze. We went to the same high school, and now he was buying ounces from me. He had always had a crush on me, but I never fucked with him. I was sure not going to fuck with him now. He was a pretty dark colored guy who was slim with a bald head and tattoos all over his body. He used to be a killer back in the day. That was why niggas trying to get on his line.

"What's good, Shantell?"

"Nothing. Hurry up and get this shit. I need to get out from back here."

"Damn, you always in a rush to leave."

"Boy, don't play with me. I 'm not trying to get shot getting caught up in your bullshit."

"Here's your money. You need to stop acting bad with me."

"Boy, whatever."

I made a couple more calls. I went home for more work and drove out to Kenner on the outskirts of New Orleans. Jackie had turned me on to a few strippers out here that moved a few ounces.

I pulled up to Pam's house. Pam ran the block in this neighborhood and sold coke, weed, and pills to the strippers.

She wanted to get down in the bed with me, but she was not a feminine bisexual. She was the boyish type, and she had a mohawk. She dressed like a boy with her pants sagging and everything. If I wanted a man, I would just fuck Darrell.

"What's going on, baby girl? You look good," she said.

"Nothing. Coolin'."

"When is your fine ass going to let me eat you out. She smiled and licked her lips.

"Girl, you crazy. Get this stuff and roll out my car."

She rolled her eyes, gave me the money and took her four ounces.

Later, I sat in the back of my shop with Keshon running the money through an automatic counter. I put her in on what was going on. I had told her I was on the verge of losing the shop when the Feds took everything. I had to do what I had to do. I told her I had found one of Keith's old stashes, and I had to make moves. I told her I would break bread with her if she would help me count the money and keep watch over the stuff in the shop.

She was down for it.

I was not going to lie. This coke shit was moving pretty good. I was making good money. Between me, Jackie and Kesha, we ran through bricks like water.

We finished counting the money and it was two hundred fifty thousand dollars. A bitch was balling for real. I'd never seen cash like this before. I called Brittney to tell her I needed fifteen kilos this time.

Chapter 20

Shantell

I was in the hotel waiting on Brittney. The guy that she was getting the coke from wanted to meet me. At first, I was spooking. I didn't want to meet nobody. I was cool with the way things were going with Brittney getting the stuff and bringing it back. I didn't want to get involved with anybody except Deloso, but I thought about it. This guy might get me close to Deloso.

Ten minutes later, Brittney and I pulled up to the Longhorn Restaurant on Westheimer waiting for Eric. A black motorbike pulled up beside us.

"That's him," Brittney said.

The brother was fine. He pulled off his helmet, and he was handsome. He looked like the supermodel Tyson Beckford. He was wearing blue jeans, white polo shirt, red light blue Timberland. He had hazel eyes and a low haircut with waves.

"What's up, Brittney?" He hugged her.

"Nothing. This is my friend, Shantell. She's the one you wanted to meet."

"Oh, yes, nice to meet you," he kissed my hand.

"Same here."

"Let's go inside and talk."

As we sat at the table eating, he asked me lots of questions. "So, you and Brittney are friends, huh?"

"Yeah, we go back to college."

"She told me that you're been moving a lot of work lately."

"A little bit."

"Who are you moving it for? Your husband?"

"No, he's in jail. I move work for myself."

"What made you start selling drugs?"

"When my husband went to prison for thirty years, the Feds took everything. I fell on hard times I need to make money to take care of me and my kids."

"Where are you moving this work at?"

"New Orleans."

"You got to be careful down there. Them niggas be killing shit. They don't play."

"I got this."

"Let's get down to business. You want to get fifteen keys."

"Yes."

"How about this? You buy fifteen, and I'll front you fifteen."

"Let me get this straight. I buy fifteen, and you're going to give me fifteen more."

"Right, and I'll give it to you for fifteen each."

I thought about it and did the math in my head. "You got a deal." We shook hands.

"Okay, this meeting is over. I got to be out. Brittney, holla at me. Shantell, it was nice to meet you."

"Same here." I smiled as I watched his ass as he walked out. "Damn, bitch. That nigga is fine. Why ain't you fucking him?"

"I fucked him a couple of times. Nothing serious. I used to move work for him back in the day. He's not the type to settle down. He's fucking too many hoes around here."

"I hear you, but his ass is fine as fuck."

I stayed in Houston a couple of more days until Eric got straight. I partied with Brittney. We balled out and had a good time. I fucked a couple of hoes out of the strip club with Brittney. When I got up the next morning, everyone was gone. When I got back from the bathroom, she came in with a black leather bag on her shoulder. She sat down on the bed and opened it.

"Bitch, this is a lot of bricks," she said.

"I see that. How the fuck am I supposed to get it back to New Orleans?"

"You me to go back with you?"

I did need someone to ride with me. I was damn sure going to be nervous."

"Okay, get your shit."

As soon as I entered Beaumont, a state trooper pulled behind us, hitting his lights.

"Shit!" I said, nervous as fuck.

138

"Bitch, be cool."

"Bitch, we got thirty bricks of coke in the trunk, or did you forget?" Butterflies filled my stomach. I felt like I was going to shit on myself. If he found it, I was just going to tell him I work for the Feds. Hopefully he could get me out this shit.

"Bitch, be cool. The majority of these niggas just want a bitch's number and to look at a bitch's titties or legs. Or they want you to get out of the car so they can feel you up. Trust me. I've been pulled over on countless occasions. I just let these motherfuckers rub on my ass."

She opened her blouse to show her titties and pulled up her dress to show off her red thong. In the rearview mirror, I saw a tall, dark-skinned brother walking toward my car. I rolled down the window as he approached my car.

"Can I help you, officer?" I asked.

"License and proof of insurance."

He looked Brittney up and down a I reached in the glove box for my insurance.

"Here you go."

"What's your name, Ms. Lady?" he asked Brittney.

"Ms. Puss."

"W-What?" he stuttered.

"I'm a stripper."

"Where at?"

"We both shake our asses at the Harlem and Dreams in Houston."

"Is that right?"

"I'll give you my number. Call me when you're in Houston."

"Come on to the back of my car."

She got out. He turned to me. "Here's your license and insurance. Slow down."

"Yes, sir."

I watched as he rubbed her on the ass and legs as she gave him her number. She got back in the car. "Come on let go."

"Damn, like that, huh?"

"I told you them niggas be easy. I might fuck him. I like him."

"Yeah, you never know when we might meet him again."

We made it to the city with no more problems. I dropped some work off at my shop. The rest we started to move.

Chapter 21

Shantell

For the next two weeks, I let Jackie handle everything. I gave her the keys and codes to all the safes. I had to spend time with my kids before they went back to school. I took them to Disneyworld in Florida. We had a ball of fun for two weeks.

I called in to check with Jackie from time to time to make sure shit was running right, but there were no problems. I left Jackie with twenty keys and had put the other ten up. I needed them to fall back on in case something went left.

On the first day of school, my phone rang as I was leaving to take my kids to school. Thank God for this dope shit because school clothes were high a s a motherfucker. I didn't pay attention to it when Keith was home. A bitch paid attention to everything when it's her own money though.

I answered the phone, and it was the federal prosecutor. "You need to come in so we can talk."

"I can be there in a couple of hours."

"See you then."

It had been more than five months since I last talked to the Feds. After dropping off the kids, I went to the federal building. I was escorted into the FDA's office.

He was talking on the phone, but hung up as I entered, "Have a seat, Ms. Washington."

I shut the door and nervously sat down. I hoped these bitches weren't calling me down here to call this shit off, or to tell me they didn't need me anymore. If so, I was going to go ham in this bitch. They were going to have to lock my black ass up today. I would be where Keith was.

"What's been going on?" he began.

"Everything's in motion."

"How close have you gotten to Deloso?"

"I met this man named Eric."

"Eric Simmons. He's the middleman for Deloso in Texas. He pushes a lot of coke for the Gulf Coast cartel in Texas."

"Damn, how do you know that?"

"We know everything. Look, you need to start buying stuff. Start acting more like a heavy weight. You know what drug dealers are like. They want to be seen."

"I got you."

"It's not like you don't have money."

"I'm on it."

I left the federal building and traded in my Bentley for a new one. I dropped a quarter million on it. I bought new Audi R8 coupes for Jackie, Kesha and Keshon. I had Brittney come over from Houston and bought her the Benz truck she had always wanted.

My crew was lit now. We were flossing all around the city making moves. We went to the Metro for Rihanna's after party. Everyone's head turned. We stepped out draped. in platinum and diamonds, wearing Fendi from head to toe. A lot of bitches were hating on us.

We walked straight into the club and went to the VIP section. We ordered bottles of Cîroc and Patron. Niggas that were trying to get weight gave us their number. Even some hoes that were balling gave their numbers. They heard a bitch had the best dope and the cheapest prices in the city.

Kesha introduced me to a couple of niggas that were pushing keys and trying to score weight. One of the niggas came in the VIP section to talk. He was brown-skinned, bald, and cute. He was dressed in black and brown Gucci from head to toe and iced out.

"Shantell, this is Ray," Kesha said.

"What's good." I said.

"I hear you're moving them things and that you have some nice prices."

"Yeah, look, it is all love, but right now I'm enjoying myself. Give Kesha your number, and I'll get up with you."

"Good looking out."

We chilled and had fun at the after party, drinking, smoking and getting fucked up.

I made it home around two o' clock and fell in the bed like a rock.

Caught Up in the Life

***

The next evening, I got up and checked my messages. All kinds of bitches and niggas were calling leaving messages. They were all trying to score. I called Eric and told him I was on my way and needed to buy fifty bricks. I asked my mother to pick up the kids from school and headed out to Houston.

As I arrived, I called Eric. He said he needed to meet with me again. We met again at Longhorn. As I walked in, I was very nervous with butterflies again. There was no need for me to see him. All I needed was to see the runner and go. I hoped this nigga hadn't found out I was working for the Feds and was about to kill me.

I should have smoked some weed or snorted some coke. At least then my nerves would be calm.

I sat down in the booth.

"How many do you think you can move?"

I breath out in relief when I heard him talk about moving keys. "So far, I can move about fifty a month."

"Okay, same deal as last time. You buy fifty, and I front you fifty. Fifteen each."

"Sure, but there's a problem. I can't get a hundred bricks in my car."

"Don't worry. I got you."

"We got a deal?"

I hit the highway in a black Yukon that Eric got for me. It had a false gas tanks on it that held a hundred bricks. I was still nervous moving that much coke, but I made it to New Orleans with no problems.

I went straight to the beauty shop where I had told the girls to meet. We gathered around the table where I had the bricks laid out.

"Bitch, this a lot of coke," Jackie said.

"Yeah, a hundred bricks. We in this shit knee deep now. If anybody wants out tell me now. Shit's about to get real, and we're about to make some real money."

"No, I'm good," Jackie said. Brittney, Kesha, and Keshon agreed.

"Keshon, just keep counting the money. The rest of you bitches, it's time to make money."

I gave each of them ten bricks and let them do their thing.

Chapter 22

Shantell

Kesha and I were counting money. I was running the last forty thousand through the machine. My phone rang.

"What's up, Ms. B?" a voice said.

"Shit, it's all good. What you need?"

"I need three bricks."

"Normal spot in thirty?"

"A'ight."

Ms. Bitch was what they called me on the streets. I was that bitch on the street because I had that work for the cheapest price. I even had product when there's a drought.

"Ke, finish this shit up. I got to go make a move."

"I got you."

I grabbed three bricks and dropped them into a Gucci bag. Before I went across the river, I had to make a quick stop to give some people work. I pulled into a gas station on MLK and waited for this fine ass stripper to meet me. Candy jumped in my car. She was light-skinned with a big, round ass, long red hair, and big red titties. She was wearing green legging, a black T-shirt and pink house shoes. She looked a bit like Draya the model.

"Hey, girl what's up?" she asked.

"Not much, just getting to this money."

"When we going to hook up again."

"I don't know. When I have the time."

"Here ten stacks."

"Look under the seat and grab the half brick."

She grabbed the coke, leaned over and kissed me on the lips. Damn. The bitch was fine and could eat some pussy. I might have to make time for her.

I pulled up to a Shoney's across the river where I met this nigga Ray. He'd been scoring bricks and half bricks from me since I met him at the club.

As the nigga walked from his car to mine, I got a feeling something wasn't right. He got in and handed me twenty grand. Against my better judgment, I served the nigga.

As I tried to pull off, the Feds rushed my car from every direction pointing their guns at me.

"Turn off the fucking car," they screamed.

I turned off the car and slowly stepped out with my hands raised. They rushed me to put me in handcuffs and pat me down. "She's clean."

They put me in the back of an FBI car. I looked at the bitch ass nigga as they let him go. Now I see why drug dealers don't trust no one. I didn't tell them I was working for the Feds. I kept my mouth closed. Let those motherfuckers figure it out.

***

They had me in an interrogation room for about forty five minutes. At first, they tried to question me and shit, but I just told them I wanted a lawyer. Eventually they came back in and uncuffed me.

"You're free to go."

I didn't ask them shit. I grabbed my purse and left.

Outside a black Cadillac truck was waiting for me. As the dark tinted windows was rolled down, I saw the prosecutor.

"Get in."

I did. "What are you doing here?"

"Getting you out of jail. Have you gotten any closer to Deloso?"

"Shit, I'm still getting work from Eric."

"How much?"

"A hundred keys."

"Just keep at it. When you get to two hundred or better, Deloso will want to talk to you."

"Okay."

"Keep me informed of your progress."

I got out of the truck and walked over to my waiting car. Good thing I was working for the Feds or my ass would be still in that bitch facing a lot of time. They gave me everything back because I was working for them. It was on now.

I couldn't believe I had a get out of jail free card. It was time to push this shit to the limit. It was time to meet Deloso.

**

At home, my phone rang. It was Darrell. I wasn't going to lie. I needed some dick. I hadn't had any in a while. I hadn't talked to him in months. I had told him we would go out when I went back to Houston.

"What's up. Haven't heard from you in a while," he said.

"Yeah, I've been working."

"When are you going to get a vacation?"

"I got to come to Houston for business. I'll call when I make it down."

Robert Baptiste

Chapter 23

Shantell

I flew into Houston and met Eric at Ruth's Chris. We sat at a table eating steak and shrimp while talking business.

"So, what's good," he asked

"I need more work."

"What we talking?"

"Like fifteen kilos."

"You can move that much?"

"Yeah, I moved a hundred in a month's time."

"Okay, I'll give you two hundred at 12.5 a key."

"I need you to get them to New Orleans for me."

"No worries."

"Good. I got to bounce. I'll see you next month."

"You didn't finish your steak."

"I got to make a move."

I jumped in my rental and called Darrell. "Hey, what's good?" he asked.

"I'm on my way."

"Sound good."

When he opened the door, I greeted him with kisses. My pussy was on fire. I needed some loving. I tore his clothes off and pushed him on the bed. I took off my clothes and climbed on top of him. I sucked his dick like it was the last one on earth, deep throating it.

I climbed on top of him and inserted his dick in my warm, wet pussy. I rode him like a thoroughbred. I bounced up and down on his dick as he grabbed my ass slamming his dick deep into me.

I learned forward digging my nails into his chest. I came back to back on his dick. He flipped me over, putting my legs over his shoulders and thrusted in and out of me. I dug my nails into his back and bit him on the shoulder.

"Fuck me, daddy."

The deeper he went the more I came. I got in a doggy-style position letting him fuck me from the back. I grabbed the sheets screaming out his name. He started shaking, and I backed my ass up on him, as he shot his hot nut in me.

We fell on the bed catching our breath, laying in our sweat and cum. Damn, I needed that.

A few hours later, Darrell got up and cooked us something to eat. I stayed over and he made love to me the whole night. I knew it was wrong. I felt guilty about, but I blocked that shit out. My body needed this.

I got up at the break of dawn, grabbed my things, and left him asleep. I'd done what I came to do. I gave him a couple of nuts and got me a couple. Fair exchange was no robbery.

Back in New Orleans, a U-Haul was waiting for me at storage. A couple of Mexicans that worked for Eric helped me unload it. I hit Eric up letting him know all was good.

Chapter 24

Shantell

The two hundred bricks were gone in less than two months, and I was calling him for more. Now I saw why niggas in the game didn't want to give it up. This game was addictive, especially the money. Getting thousands at a time and turning them into millions was a high. You could buy whatever you wanted whenever you wanted.

My clientele was going through the roof. I had the cheapest prices in the city, and the best product on the market. I had different niggas and hoes working for me. I had trap houses all over the city and the outskirts. I had coke in every project. Also, I had niggas hating on me because I was a bitch moving major weight through the city.

My whole team was eating good, riding good, and living good. I was driving though my kingdom when my phone rang.

"I need some money."

"Where are you?"

"Home."

"I'm going to stop by. I got you."

A few minutes later, I pulled up at Icy's house and blew the horn. We'd started back fucking around after she broke up with her boyfriend. She was my side piece. When I needed someone to get me off and I couldn't reach Darrell, I called her. She fell on hard times after breaking up with her boyfriend, so I'd been looking out for her. I threw her some money and took her shopping. She didn't know about the drug stuff, and I wasn't going to tell her.

My business wasn't for everyone.

She ran outside wearing tight blue shorts that were riding up in her ass, a black and pink T-shirt and black house slippers. Her hair was in a ponytail.

"Hey, girl," she said, leaning over and kissing me.

"What's up with you? You need a whole makeover."

"I know I need it. I've been going through a lot, you know."

"I understand. Don't trip though. I got you." I gave her five stacks.

"Something to hold you over. I told you I got you."

"Thanks. I love you."

"Get in the car. We're going to the mall for that make over."

I took her to a salon for the works. I spent ten grand on her. We left the mall, went back to my house and fucked and sucked each other to death.

***

The next morning, I looked over at Icy's fine ass while she was sleeping. As I checked my messages, I saw Eric had called five times I wondered what he wanted. I got the load for the month already. Every time he called me without me having to call him, I worried that this nigga found out I was working for the Feds.

I called his number. "What's up, E?"

"We need to talk. When can you come down?"

"Today, if it's important."

"It is."

"I'll be there this afternoon." I hoped he just wanted to talk about the three hundred bricks I need.

I got dressed, kissed Icy and told her she could stay since the kids were with my mother. Then I took off for Houston. I phoned Jackie on the way. "I got to go to Houston. Eric wants to talk."

"About what? We got work."

"I told you I was trying to line up three hundred bricks."

"Handle your business, bitch. I'll hold things down here 'til you get back."

"I'll let you know what happens."

"Be safe. Love you."

I got a seat on the first available flight. As soon as we landed, Darrell hit me up on the phone. I had been ignoring him the last few months. I really didn't want to get involved with him. I needed to stay focused on the task at hand and that was to get close to this cartel motherfucker, so I could get my husband out of prison.

But a bitch's pussy was talking to her, and getting it sucked didn't get it done like it used to. I needed some good dick. Nothing could replace that.

"Long time no hear from. I could've thought you were ducking me," Darrell said.

"No, it's not like that. My mother has been sick." The lie came to me quickly.

"Damn, sorry to hear it. I hope she's getting better."

"Thanks."

"When are you going to come see me?"

"I was just going to call you when you called me. I just got in town."

"For real?"

"Yeah, I got a little business. We can hang after that."

"Sound great."

"I was thinking about spending the weekend with you."

"Works for me."

"I'll call you in a little while."

After I hung, I called Eric. "Are you in town yet?" he asked.

"You want me to meet you at our normal spot?"

"No, I need you to meet me in Katy."

"Give me the directions." I grew nervous as I wondered why he wanted me to go to a house in Katy. He'd never invited me before. Maybe I would finally meet Deloso.

I saw *Goodfellas*. They killed the guy they invited to the house. Lord, I hoped this shit was not that. It was too late to turn back now.

I soon pulled up to a beautiful red, brick house. Eric was outside waiting on me. I put on a fake smile as I walked over to him. He wasn't smiling at all. I knew shit was real.

"Shantell, come with me."

"Nice house."

As we entered the house two men grabbed me and put a black bag over my head. I tried to kick and fight, but it was no use. They had me. "What kind of fucking game is this?" I screamed at Eric.

"It's going to be okay."

I was scared to death. A thousand ways to die ran through my mind. Maybe they found out I was working for the Feds, and I was about to die. Tears were running down my face. I thought about my husband and kids. I realized I should have listened to him. Now, my husband was in prison, and my mother was getting old, so who was going to raise my kids? They'd go to foster care. I cried hard.

They picked me up and put me in a van. I started praying, asking God to watch over my kids, to expect my soul, and forgive my sins. I sucked it up. I was ready for my punishment.

The van stopped. I was pulled from it. "Take this shit off me," I screamed.

No one answered.

They put me in a car and drove me for what felt like hours. I had stopped crying and was ready to face the music.

When we finally stopped, I was escorted from the car. The hood was removed, and I saw a short Mexican man wearing brown cowboy boots. He was dressed like a cowboy in blue jeans, a blue Western shirt, and brown cowboy hat. He had a thick mustache and smoked a cigar.

I had finally met Deloso.

I looked around. We were in the middle of nowhere. It looked like the desert. The only thing around seemed to be tall brown bushes. Sand was blowing everywhere. I had seen enough mob movies to know how this was going to end. Motherfuckers got killed and buried in places like this. I wasn't going to beg for my life. I put myself in this situation. I had to live with the consequences of my actions.

There were about fifty men standing around armed with Ak-47s.

"Sorry about the crude treatment, but it's necessary. That is how I make sure the Feds don't know how to get out here."

When he mentioned the Feds, I wanted to shit on myself. I knew I was dead. I just wanted him to stop stalling and get this shit over with. This motherfucker looked like one that was not to be fucked with. Now I saw why my husband didn't want to tell on this motherfucker. Fuck, I was in this shit too deep now.

"Come, let's go for a ride."

He led me to a black 550 Benz and got in. We took off. I was not going to lie. I was still nervous as shit. I didn't even want to look this motherfucker in the face. One word from him, and your life was over.

"It's okay. Relax. You've not in any danger." He spoke perfect English. "I hear you're from New Orleans."

I nodded, still too nervous to speak.

"I had a connect in New Orleans back in the day. I heard he was busted and got thirty years with the Feds. If he gets out, I'll look out for him since he kept it real with me. He didn't talk. I respect that. He could have brought me down. I made sure the motherfucker that informed on him was dead."

When he talked about my husband, I swallowed hard. Keith must have never told him about his family because if he had, he would have put two and two together, and I'd be dead.

"I hear you've been moving a lot of my coke."

"Y... yes sir. That's right."

"Now, you want three hundred kilos."

"That's correct." I found my voice a bit when he talked about serving coke. I knew I was good.

"This is where I live," he said as he rolled down the windows. I saw a white rail fence running around a big, white brick mansion that looked like it was out of *Scarface*. Workers ran around like ants. The house sat on five thousand acres of land.

We got out of his car and were greeted by a Mexican maid. "Can I get you something to drink?" she asked.

"Some water, please." A bitch's mouth was dry as fuck. I really wanted her to bring me a shot of Jack and a blunt. My nerves were shot to pieces. I needed to make this deal. I was hoping this would be my only trip out here. I was going to give his ass to the Feds and get this done. They could handle it from here on out, and I would get my husband back.

The living room was laid in marble and wood grain floor. This motherfucking house was laid out with crystal and marble and lots of antique furniture.

We walked to the bar and Deloso poured himself a drink. The maid returned with my water. "Thank you." I told her.

He went to his antique cherry desk, opened a box of cigars, cut one and lit it.

"Come on. I want to show you something."

We walked out to his barn. There were horses there.

"Are these racehorses?" I asked.

Robert Baptiste

"Yes, the finest and fastest in the world. I paid ten million each for them, but I don't race them. I use them for breeding. Each ounce of semen is worth two hundred thousand dollars."

We went to the other side of the barn. There were butt naked woman making bricks of cocaine. He put his hands into one of the barrels. It was filled with nothing but crystal.

"This is pure. The best cocaine money can buy. It's never even been stepped on once. Straight off the leaf. Let's go back inside."

We sat in his living room sipping a vintage red wine. "Here's the deal. You want to buy three hundred keys. I'll give you five hundred at ten grand each. You only work for me. I need a new dealer in New Orleans. I will provide directly. I'll get it delivered where you need it every month. What do you say?"

All I saw were dollars signs. Five hundred keys a month at ten a key. Fuck, that was a lot of money. A deal like this made me not want to tell the Feds I met up with Deloso. For real, I thought about keeping this to myself. I would make as much money as I could, then tell the Feds. That way, I'll be straight when Keith got out of jail.

"How could I pass up a deal like that?" We shook hands.

"Let me know where to make the delivery."

They blindfolded me and drove me back to Eric's house. I called Jackie and told her to rent another storage space.

Then I called Darrell. After all this shit, I needed some good loving. He met me at the door, and we kissed. He carried me into the kitchen and put me on top of the counter. He tore my thong off and slide his nine-inch dick inside me. I put my legs on his shoulders as he thrusted hard into my soaking wet pussy as I held on for dear life.

"Fuck, oh yeah, give me that dick! Don't stop. I'm cuming all over your dick!" The more I talked, the deeper and harder he pounded me out. He carried me to the bedroom.

I got on top of him riding him in a reverse cowgirl. He grabbed my ass, bouncing it on his dick.

"Yeah! Ride daddy's dick! I'm cuming!"

I bounced even harder as we both started to shake. We came together. I came hard as he shot his warm nut all in me. Then I fell back and lay in his arms.

156

Chapter 25

Shantell

I awoke the next morning to breakfast in bed. Darrell made grits, sausage, sunny side up eggs, and strawberries in a bowl. He served it with freshly squeezed orange juice and milk.

"Good morning, sunshine," he greeted me.

"You shouldn't have."

"Anything for you." He left but quickly returned with a single, white rose.

"For, you."

"Thanks, but you shouldn't have." It had been a long time since a man gave me flowers. I saw where this was going, and I didn't want to go there. "Everything is nice, but I got to go." I got up to look for my clothes.

"Why are you always in a rush to leave?" He grabbed me to keep me from putting on my shirt.

"Darrell, I don't want to hurt your feelings. I don't want a relationship. It's cool the way we are. I come to town. You get you, and I get me. I'm fine with that."

"Sit down."

I sat on the bed butt naked.

"You are special to me. I haven't found a woman like you since my wife died. I don't want to be your jump off. I want us to be in a relationship."

Before I could respond his tongue was in my mouth and his dick was inside of me. I held on tight as he thrusted in and out.

"I love you," he said.

I dug my nails into his back, cuming hard back to back on his dick.

"I love you too."

I spent a couple of more days with Darrell. We went out and saw a movie. I hadn't been on a date in a while. It felt good. I missed all that. He kept asking me to take it to the next level. If I wasn't married, he'd be a perfect candidate. He was loving, romantic, and passionate. Just what I liked in a man. He reminded me of Keith. That was why I was attracted to him. I thought I might even be falling in love.

I can't let my feelings get in the way thought. I had something I had to do. I had to stay focused.

***

I hit the highway about six that afternoon. I called Deloso and set up the delivery. I saw that I had missed several calls from Brittney and Kesha. I hoped nothing bad had happened. I called Brittney.

"Where the hell have you been? I've tried to reach you for two days. You wouldn't answer your phone."

"Slow down. What's going on?"

"Jackie's in the hospital."

"What? For what?"

"Some nigga robbed her and took five kilos of dope. He beat her up, broke her arm and fucked up her face.

"I'm on my way right fucking now." I hung up to drive. As soon as I got back to the city, I went straight to the hospital. As I entered her room, I saw all the bandages. Her eyes were closed. I kissed her forehead, and she woke up.

"Jackie, I'm here. Sorry this happened to you."

"It's okay."

"I got you. I'm going to get the motherfucker who did this to you. I promise you that."

"I know who it was."

"Who?"

"This nigga name Joe."

"Where does he hang out?"

"Around the strip club."

"You get some sleep and get better. I'll handle that nigga for you." I kissed her again.

Leaving the hospital, I was as mad as a pit bull in a skirt. I couldn't let this shit slide. I had to act like Larry Fishburne in *Deep Cover* and take care of business. I needed niggas and hoes out here to know not to fuck with my crew.

The streets watched to see what you were going to do. If they thought your crew was soft, they'd try you every time. I jumped in my car and called Icy. "I need you to do me a favor."

"Meet me at my house in an hour."

Soon, Icy and I made a plan at my table.

"I need you to set this nigga up for me. He hurt my friend real bad."

"Whatever you need."

"This nigga hangs at this strip club called She She in the east. You know the strip club?"

"No problem. What does he look like?"

I went through Jackie's phone and found a picture.

"Okay, I'm on his line," she said

"I need you to bring him to the motel on Chef. I'll do the rest."

"Say no more."

"I got something for you when it's finished."

I looked at her and took a deep breath. "I need to tell you something." I put my hands on her shoulder. I took a seat on her lap and took another deep breath. "Look, I sell drugs."

"What?"

"I'm a drug dealer. I move a lot of coke."

"When did you start?"

"After Keith went to jail."

"Why are you telling me now?"

"That's what this is about. Somebody robbed my friend. Now, I got to get them back. I don't want you going in this shit blind."

"It's all good. I'm not tripping. I kind of figured you were doing something anyway. The way you taking care of me and all."

"Good looking out." I tongue kissed her.

***

I had different bitches in the strip club looking for this fool. I had a reward of twenty grand on his head. As I drove around the city, Icy hit me up.

"We about to go to the motel in a little bit. The Red Rooster Inn."

"You got him?"

"Yeah, his thirsty ass wasn't hard to find. He like to play the club and fuck the strippers."

"On my way."

I had decided I was going to kill him. Killing someone was like walking on ants, but it needed to be done.

I made it to the hotel before them. They pulled in the lot in a red 550 Benz and went to a nearby room. I gave them a few minutes to get comfortable. I let her suck his dick or fuck him. The element of surprise was a motherfucker.

I got of my car, nervous as a rmotherfucker. Icy had left the door cracked. My heart was beating wildly in my chest. I felt like I was about to shit. As I pushed the door open, she was riding him. He saw me lift the gun in the mirror. He pushed her off and reached for his gun, I knew it was either him or me.

I was scared as shit.

I just pulled the trigger hitting him six times in the chest. I kept clicking the gun, hoping he was dead. His body lay on the bed with his eyes staring at me.

"Come on," Icy said.

I came out of my daze and ran out the door behind her. We jumped in my car and pulled off. My adrenaline was racing. I had seen enough cop shows to know I needed to get rid of everything.

As I crossed the bridge, I threw the gun into the Mississippi.

Back at the shop, we changed clothes. I burned the ones we had been wearing and threw the ashes into the landfill.

Back home, we sat on my couch drinking and smoking. We didn't say a word for a long while. Finally, she looked me in the eyes and grabbed my hands. "This is our secret. I won't tell nobody. You can trust me." She leaned in and kissed me.

I led her to the bedroom without words. We had sex with each other over and over again.

Chapter 26

Shantell

I got up the next day and checked the news. The murder I'd committed wasn't mentioned, but the word was on the street. Don't miss with Ms. Bitch's workers. Respect was all you got in these streets. Without it you didn't have shit. Now, I saw why my husband was rocking the way he was. It was hard to be a dealer in the game. You had to put in work, or a mothefucker was going to be testing you.

I picked Jackie up from the hospital. Her face was back to normal, but her arm wasn't.

"I handled that business for you."

"Thank you. I love you."

"I told you I got you. Let's go home."

We pulled up to her house in Eastover, just down the street from mine. I had gotten my old house back. It had been in foreclosure. I paid a lawyer to put it in his name. I paid less for it than it costed my husband to build it. It cost one and a half million to build, but I only paid nine hundred thousand to get it back.

Jackie was surprised by the gift in her driveway. It was a red Maserati with a big red bow on top. "I know that's not for me," she said with tears running down her face.

"Yeah, I told you I got you."

She hugged me then went over and looked at the car. I handed her the keys. She hugged me again, and we walked up to her house.

"Surprise!" everyone yelled.

"You shouldn't have." She teared up.

Kesha, Brittney, and Ke'shon came up and hugged and kissed her. We sat at her house smoking, drinking and just kicking it. I had bought the whole crew houses back here I even put Icy on the payroll and helped her get a new house. She didn't have to do shit except be my side piece.

***

In the months after the killing my clientele went through the roof. Everybody was scoring from me. I was the main supplier in the city. I had the best coke and cheapest prices.

I put together a team and had niggas and hoes working for me in my trap houses all over the city. From uptown to downtown and even across the river. We were moving a thousand bricks. I bought in teams of killers to watch our backs. I was making so much money, I bought a new house in English Turn for five million. Nothing but rich white people stayed back there. I had a Lambo and a Ferrari. I spent millions on jewelry and clothes. I took my kids on shopping sprees and brought my mother a new house.

When she asked where the money was coming from, I told her the Feds gave me Keith's money back.

We were living the American dream for real. I had money in different overseas banks. I was living like *Scar Face*. I was the number one drug dealer in the city like Deloso told me I would be.

That was why it was hard to meet with the prosecutor. I sat in his office draped in about two million dollars from head to toe.

"What's been happening? I haven't seen you in a while. I hear you're moving a lot of drugs on the streets, Ms. Bitch. I see you've opened large overseas accounts. It must feel good living the rich life. Just like you lived when your husband was out."

"I'm doing what you told me. Just living like a drug dealer."

"How close are you to Deloso?"

I had to think fast. I wasn't ready to give up all this shit yet. "I'm still copping from Eric. He won't plug me in with him yet."

"Tell him you need to score even more. He'll meet you then."

I jumped in my car and drove off. He must think I'm an idiot. I wouldn't give Deloso up right off the bat. I wanted my husband home, but it could wait a little. I wanted to build up cash, so he wouldn't want for anything. I had too much going on to give everything up. I couldn't give up making millions a week and my respect in the streets. We went from a thousand kilos to fifteen kilos in storage. The Feds would take everything once I busted Deloso, but Deloso has been good to me. My friends and family were straight. I was making millions every week. I wasn't about to bring that to an end.

Caught Up in the Life

Fuck! They must have me fucking confused with somebody stupid.

Robert Baptiste

Chapter 27

Shantell

We were at one of my condos uptown running money through the machine. I needed to get Deloso's money to him. I liked being on time with it. My name was popping on the streets, and I put a lot of niggas and bitches on. My life had really changed. I was no longer a simple housewife who owned a beauty supply store. I had five salons, all in the different cities.

My whole attitude about the streets had changed. I was a real boss bitch who didn't play when it came to my money. One bitch who worked for me kept coming up short. I felt this bitch was playing me. And after I put the broke hoe on and let her eat. The bitch was taking my kindness for weakness. The bitch thinks I'm a motherfucking joke. I watched that bitch, Day, walk in the room. Day was dark-skinned and slim with purple weave in her hair. When she stripped, she was always broke. I felt sorry for the bitch, so I put her on to moving coke.

"What's up? You got my money?"

"Yeah, but I'm a couple thousand short."

Before I knew it, I jumped up and hit the bitch in the mouth with a quick back hand. She fell to the floor, and I went to stomping her ass out. I kicked her in the face and stomach.

"Bitch, you better get my money. I don't give a fuck how you do it."

Jackie grabbed my arm, but I pulled away. "This bitch always corning up short." I kicked her in the face again.

"Damn, bitch. You fucked her up," Jackie said.

I looked at her bleeding everywhere. "Are we still going out tonight?" I sat back down and hit a blunt like nothing had happened.

"Yeah, we still going out," Jackie said.

"Okay," I put up the money and the dope up. "Let's get out of here."

"Now, get this bitch out of here. I'm out. Call and tell me where to meet you."

As I was getting in the shower, I decided I needed to get out of town. I wanted to see some butt naked hoes. I was tired of going out into the city and seeing the same niggas and hoes. The city to see some fine ass, butt naked hoes was Atlanta.

I called the airport and chartered a plane. That was the least I could do for them with the way they hustled for me.

I put on my red Chanel dress with my white Chanel stiletto boots. I wore million-dollar diamond earrings as well as a diamond necklace and watch. My hair was hanging long because it was freshly permed.

After a quick mirror check I grabbed my red ten thousand dollar Chanel purse, jumped in my pink McLaren and pulled out of the driveway. After picking up the girls, we went to the airport. A short while later we were in Atlanta.

At the airport, I had a black Mercedes-Benz Atlas touring coach van waiting for us. We started partying drinking and smoking before we even got to the strip club

We went to the Blue Fame. Thick, naked, fine bitches were shaking their asses everywhere. I went straight to the bar to get thirty thousand dollars in ones. This bitch was off the chain. All types of rappers and basketball niggas were here. We went to the VIP where I had them bring bottles of Cîroc. All kinds of bad bitches came and joined us. They gave us lap dances, and we threw money at those fine hoes. I even saw one of my best friends from high school.,

"Hey, Taraji long time bitch," I said,

"Hey, Shantell, bitch."

We hugged each other tight.

"Bitch, it been a long time," I said.

"Sure have. What you doing out here?" she asked

"Coolin' with a couple of my home girls, and you?"

"Me and my husband just came out to chill. He play for the Hawks."

"A rich nigga, huh?"

"Bitch, you know how I get down."

"I ain't mad at you."

Taraji was a cold-blooded hood bitch, but the hoe only dated ballers and NBA players. She was high yellow, Creole with long, black, wavy hair. Honey was fine as fuck with a big ass. It was not fake. It ran in her family. Them niggas thought they had something special, but that hoe been run through. She was my dog though. I didn't knock her.

"Bitch, I'm about to go."

"Here put my number in your phone and call me," I said. We hugged.

I woke up the next morning at the Four Seasons with a hangover. I looked around the suite. There were naked hoes everywhere. It was like there had been an orgy in this motherfucker. I'd had so much weed and Cîroc that I didn't even remember the night before.

I checked my phone. I had missed a few calls but nothing important. Keith was in the hole. He and his cellmate got busted with some knives in the cell. My mother had the kids, so it was all good. I decided to stay and chill for a week.

I threw on a pink jogging suit with some white Air Jordan's and left those hoes to sleep it off. I went to the underground mall to cop me a few things and check it out. When I got back all the stripper hoes were gone.

"Bitch, where you been?" Brittney asked

"At the mall."

"And you couldn't take us," Jackie said as she walked out of the bathroom.

"No, you hoes were knocked out."

"Light something up," Kesha said.

"Please," Icy added.

"Bitch, I had fun last night." Brittney smiled.

"It was off the chain," they said at the same time while dapping each other up.

"Bitch, I was so high and drunk, I don't remember shit."

"You should. You're the one that bought all the bitches back to the hotel. We had a orgy," Brittney said.

"Stop lying."

"Bitch, you were an animal on the Cîroc," Brittney agreed.

"Fuck it. Blame it on the alcohol." I smiled.

We spent the whole week touring the city, taking pictures, and hitting the major clubs and strip clubs.

* * *

When we made it back home, my phone was blowing up with different people needing work. I called Dave back. Dave was one of few people I served. I didn't serve anyone unless they got at least twenty kilos. All I really did was ride around, collect money, and made sure everything was good for the workers.

"Hey, Dave. What's up?"

"I need about thirty of them things."

"Meet you at the spot."

I went to a stash house and picked up thirty bricks. I soon got to his barber shop on Downman in New Orleans East. I went in with the two bags and walked straight to his office. He hung up the phone as I entered.

Dave was brown-skinned and about 5'8. He looked like Michael B. Jordan. He liked to flirt every time we did business, but I would never mess with him. He was married. Plus, I didn't play games. It was in and out, strictly business.

"Come on, man. Let's do this," I said, stacking the bricks on the table.

"Why you always act that way with me. Chill for a minute."

"Man, run me my money, so I can be out. I don't have time for bullshit today."

I took the three hundred thousand dollars and stuffed it in my bad. I bounced without saying a word. I dropped the money off at the money house and checked a couple of trap houses. I picked up money and made sure they had product and that they were straight.

I had been paying Baldwin money to keep his mouth shut and handle my legal affairs. I knew he talked to Keith from time to time about the appeal. If he ever told Keith what I was doing, he knew I would get his ass killed.

As I drove home, Darrell called. "Hey, boo," I said.

"What's good? When are you coming down?"

"I've been thinking about you. My body need some good loving. I'll be there in a couple of days."

"All right, I love you."

"Love you back."

I needed to make a run to Houston to see Deloso. We had semi-regular meetings at his house for his major dealers. It was just informational. He told us what we needed to know and made sure things were running smoothly.

Robert Baptiste

Chapter 28

Shantell

I pulled up to a mansion on the northside of Houston. As I got out of the car, a guard patted me down.

The mansion was decked out in marble, crystal and fine woods. The guard booked me to a conference room. There was a large table and big black leather chairs.

The chairs were filled by people from all over the country. He supplied people of every different race, both men and women. I faked a smile at everyone as I waited for Deloso to come in. It was quiet as shit. You could hear a rat piss on cotton.

I was not going to lie. I was nervous as fuck. I'd never been to nothing like this before.

Deloso came in dressed in a black suit and carrying a baseball bat. He went to the head of the table and looked everyone in the face. His bodyguards closed the doors as they entered the room. They stood there with their guns in their hands.

"Someone hasn't been playing fair." He started walking around the table, swinging the bat into his hand. "Someone at this table is talking to the Feds."

My heart dropped to my ass when he said that.

"You know what I do to people who talk to the Feds. Moreover, my money has been short. Two things I don't play about is my money and the Feds."

He stopped at my chair. My armpits were sweating, and my heart was racing. I gripped the chair tightly, trying to prepare myself for the worst.

He cocked the bat back and slammed in into the head of the Mexican guy beside me.

I about shitted on myself. I know I farted.

I watched the blood explode from his head. It hit me and Deloso. The man's head was on the table. His eyes were open. Deloso continued to hit him. It fucked me up.

He finally stopped hitting him. "I hate snitches and thieves." He called a bodyguard over. "Give Ms. B a gun. I need her to finish this pig."

I took the gun and looked at the barely breathing man. I knew I couldn't hesitate or say I wouldn't do it because I would find my ass on the other end of the stick.

So, I shot the guy in the head to put him out of his misery.

Everybody had to take the gun and shoot him, so nobody would know which bullet killed him. We all had blood on our hands.

"Get him the fuck out of here. Kill his entire fucking family. I want everybody dead." Deloso turned back to us. "Let this be a warning. Don't try to fuck me over, or you'll end up like that motherfucker. He worked for me for twenty years. We grew up together. Meeting is over. See you in a month."

I jumped in my car wondering just what the fuck I'd gotten myself into, or worse, my family. I saw why Keith didn't want to tell on this motherfucker because he didn't play.

I met Darrell at a bar. I immediately ordered two Patron shots and hit them straight.

"Are you all right?" he asked as I took two more shots.

"I just saw my life flash in front of me."

"What happened?"

"An eighteen-wheeler almost hit me." I lied.

"Sorry. I'm glad you're okay."

"Me too."

We chilled, talked, and drank for a while. We headed over to his place and fucked all night. I lay my head on his chest to listen to his heartbeat.

"I've been thinking." He ran his fingers through my hair.

"About what?"

"You moving here with me."

"My family isn't here."

"We could get a house together wherever you went. I don't have a problem moving. We need to take our relationship to the next level. We've dated for a year and half. You love me, right?"

"But, but…"

172

"But what? If I love you and you love me, there should be no buts. I'm tired of waking up with you not here. This long-distance relationship is for the birds. So, what do you say?"

"I feel the same way, but I need to think about it. I'll get back to you." I kissed him.

I got up the next morning and looked at him sleeping. I knew my feelings were growing stronger. I wanted to tell him my secret, but the time wasn't right.

I grabbed my clothes, kissed him on the forehead and hit the interstate.

Robert Baptiste

Chapter 29

Shantell

As I was driving back to the city, I thought about Darrell and the conversation we had the night before. I was in love with him. He was a good man. He was also in love with me. I had fallen for him.

I couldn't keep lying to myself. Keith had thirty years in the Feds, and my feeling were moving on from him. Maybe Jackie was right. Maybe I needed to let Keith go and move on with my life.

My musing was interrupted by the phone. "We got a problem," Keshon said.

Damn, every time I go out of town these bitches get into shit. "What's going on?"

"Brittney's been kidnapped, and Kesha' s in jail."

"Shit! What?"

"They called and said they want a million dollars and ten bricks for her."

"Fuck. All right. I'm coming in the city now. Bond Kesha out."

"All right."

I wondered who in the fuck was playing with me like this. Their ass was dead when I found out who they were.

As I was about to get off the bridge, a truck pulled up alongside me and began shooting into my car. Several bullets hit my door, and glass exploded in my face. I swerved and hit the guide rail on the side of the bridge. Thank God, it was there, or my ass would have gone over it.

My car flipped three times. Broken glass hit me repeatedly. I felt my airbag hit me in the face. Before I passed out, two guys got out of the truck and ran toward my car with guns in hand.

***

I awoke five hours later in a frantic state at the hospital. I had tubes coming from everywhere. As the doctor came in, I checked myself for bullet holes. I didn't find any to my surprise.

"You're lucky. You probably should be dead," the doctor said.

"I need some Aspirin. I have a headache."

"W'ell get some. You have some damage to the skull. It looks like it's mostly bruises and scrapes. We need to keep you overnight for observation."

"Sorry, doc. I can't do that. I got things to do." I started pulling tubes from my arms and tried to stand up. I was lightheaded and fell back on the bed unconscious.

I woke up two hours later to see Jackie standing over me rubbing my head. "How are you feeling?"

"Okay! I guess."

"You're better than your car. It has like a thousand bullet holes in it. God must have been with you."

"Did they call you about Brittney?"

"Yeah, now they want two million for her. They gave us two hours to get it, or they're going to kill her."

"I need you to help me get out of this hospital."

"Are you sure?"

"Yeah, ain't no telling when these motherfuckers may try to come in here and get me."

"Do you know who they are?"

"No, I got to figure it out."

Jackie helped me get out of bed. I was still a little lightheaded, but I didn't pass out this, time. We drove to my shop. I put two million dollars into four bags. "Did you get Kesha out of jail?" I asked Jackie.

"Yeah, I've been trying to hit her up, but she ain't called back yet."

"Let's swing through the project."

Jackie and I got to her apartment. The door was cracked open, and everything was trashed. As we walked through the house. I saw her feet hanging out of the bathroom door.

Kesha was lying on her back dead. She'd been shot twice in the head. She was naked and had been raped.

"What the fuck happened?" Jackie began to cry.

"Go find a sheet." I fell to the floor as she left. Crying, I picked up her head and kissed her. "I'm sorry I wasn't there for you, but I will make those motherfuckers pay for this."

Jackie came back and handed me a sheet. I covered her. Jackie and I went through the house looking for the money and drugs.

"Shit, they took it all," she said.

"Let's be out."

We wiped everything down and left. I called the police to report it.

As we left, those motherfuckers called Jackie's phone. "This is them right chere."

"Answer it."

"Hello."

"You got the money?" the voice asked.

"Yes."

"Come to the blue warehouse in the warehouse district."

"We're on the way." She hung up.

"What did they say?"

"They want to meet at the blue warehouse."

Jackie and I arrived at the warehouse shortly. My team was there on standby. What? You didn't think I'd come without my team, or that I was going to give them niggas two million dollars, did you?

They pulled up to the loading dock door, and we pulled in. We got out of the car with bags in hands as they got out of the van wearing masks.

"Where's my best friend?" I asked.

"Where's the money?"

"Right chere."

"Slide it over."

"I need to see my friend first."

They pulled her from the van. She had duct tape on her hands and mouth. "Now slide the money over here."

"We'll do it at the same time."

I slid the bag to them as they let her go. As she was running to us, I saw them pull guns. Jackie and I pulled our guns out and started shooting.

My team rushed in and went to shooting. After our exchange of fire we killed those motherfuckers. I went and pulled the mask off. One was the young nigga out the Magnolia that I was serving. I shot the nigga twice in the head just for the fuck of it.

We left and went home. I thought about my near death and Kesha's murder. I got in the shower and fell down crying over Kesha. I saw why Keith was the way he was in the streets. In the city of New Orleans, you had to be a killer. You can't show no weakness. You were either a wolf or a sheep. The Bible said that you can't be a sheep among the wolves.

After getting out of the shower, I called Kesha's mother to tell her the news. I told her that if she needed anything, I had her. Kesha's death made me reflect on my life. I hadn't been going to see Keith like I should've. I haven't even been spending time with my kids.

I decided I would go visit Keith the next day.

***

At the prison, I checked in and waited for Keith to come in. I decide I needed to bring the kids to see him. They're older now; they're getting so big.

We hugged and kissed. He looked like he was stressed. He was starting to get a little gray hair. He had been gone for six years now. It seemed like it been longer than that. I got him some chicken wings and a Coke from the machines.

"What's up with you? Looks like you've been stressing. You got gray hair and stuff."

"No, a nigga's just getting old. That's all. I've been chilling. Waiting on my appeal. It in the Supreme Court right now. What's up with you? You ain't been up here to see a nigga."

"I been busy. I've opened a couple of salons."

"That's what up."

"Yeah, just making some moves."

"When are you going to bring the kids to see me?"

"I might do it when they get out of school."

"I know you got someone else. I want you to keep it real with me. It's cool."

I thought about telling him the truth about me and Darrell, but no man wanted to hear about another man fucking his wife. I did what any wife would do. I lied. "Yeah, Icy and I are in a relationship. We still fucking around. I told you before. This is still your pussy."

"I hear you."

As we were taking pictures, I began to feel sick to my stomach. I was happy when they ended visitation.

As I got to my car, I went to throwing up. Those fucking chicken wings had me feeling fucked up. I threw up again.

It took forever, but I finally made it home. I lay in bed, nauseous. As I threw up again, I remembered the last time I felt this way.

"Fuck no! Fuck no! I can't be. I can't be," I wailed aloud.

I grabbed a pregnancy test and pissed on it. I was pregnant. I took another one. Positive again. I needed to make an appointment with a doctor and get rid of this motherfucker Immediately. I wasn't going to bring another man's baby into the world while I was still married. Fuck no. That wasn't going to happen. He'd kill my ass for sure.

Robert Baptiste

Chapter 30

Shantell

Two weeks later, I attended Kesha' s funeral. I gave her mother three million dollars for the kids. After it was over, I hugged and kissed her mother and her kids.

It broke my heart to see them like that. It made me think about my own kids. Kesha's mother was merely an older version of Kesha. I thought about her having to raise her young grandkids. I hoped and prayed that nothing would happen to me. I didn't know if my mother could take it. She'd probably lost her mind.

"Ms. Smith, if you need anything at all just call. I mean anything." I hugged her again.

I walked over to the rest of my crew. "Did you'll hear anything yet?"

They all said no.

"Keep your ears to the ground."

I got in my car and went to the doctor's office. I hadn't told anyone about the pregnancy. I didn't need people trying to talk me out of an abortion. This is a secret I will take to my grave.

I thought about who killed Kesha. I still didn't know. I didn't know who had tried to kill me that day either. One motherfucker was on my mind, but I needed to be sure. I had a hundred thousand dollars on the streets for anyone who told me what I needed to know.

Man, this drug dealing shit is for real. The more I stayed in this fucking game, the more I understood my husband's position. You know what was craziest. You could see all the bullshit, but money overrode it. It made a motherfucker want to stay in the game.

At the doctor's office, I looked around to see if I recognized anyone. If I did, I was going to walk straight out of this bitch. The last thing I needed was for one of these hoes to recognize me and go running their mouth in the streets. You know shit traveled fast in the streets, especially when a bitch is trying to keep a secret.

I walked over to the receptionist with my shades on and signed the clipboard. I chose a doctor in Slidell, a city on the outskirts of New

Orleans. While waiting, I played on my phone, mainly messing with Facebook. I waited impatiently for my name to be called.

About thirty minutes later, a nurse called out my name. The doctor was an older, white lady. "How are you doing? My name is Dr. Sanders."

"Nice to meet you." We shook hands.

It was cold in the examination room. I was nervous as hell. I had never done some shit like this before. I should have brought someone with me.

"Get up on the table," the doctor told me. She rolled her chair closer to me.

"Ms. Washington. Why are you here today?"

"I need to have an abortion."

"Are you sure?"

"Yes."

"We'll have to see how advanced the pregnancy is. Then, we'll talk."

"Okay."

I removed my clothes and lay down on the table. She conducted the examination. I certainly hoped, I wasn't too far along because I would be fucked.

"It looks like you're about five weeks."

I thought, *Thank you! Jesus.*

"Are you certain you want to do the procedure?"

"Yes."

"Sign this form, and we'll start."

I went home from the clinic and cried. I couldn't stop thinking about the baby I had gotten rid of. I cried myself to sleep.

A couple of hours later, my phone woke me up. I answered it still half asleep.

"Where are you? I been calling for hours." Jackie said.

"Sorry. It's that time of month. What's going on?"

"Word on the streets is that some nigga named Fire killed and robbed Kesha. Him and some of his boys."

"Okay, we about to get his ass. Meet me at the shop."

"No, we got his ass already. Come to the warehouse."

When I walked in the warehouse, he was duct taped and bleeding from the mouth and head. The men who helped him were already killed and lying on the floor.

"So, you're the little nigga that killed my friend? I know you ass was going to be trouble when I first seen you in the project. I should've got rid of your ass then." I looked him over.

"Fuck you, bitch. I'm not scared to die."

I slapped him in the face. Then I shot him in the head.

"Burn their asses. Then, dump them in the river."

As I left the warehouse, I felt a little better, but I still needed to know who put the hit on me.

I found out the afternoon while we were counting money. Mark, a hitman who had put in work for me, called. He had found out that Blaze put the hit on me. He got him a connect out of Houston and tried to get rid of me so he could take over the city. But I put them dogs on his ass.

A couple of hours later, Mark called back. "It's done."

"Good work," I said.

I had found out where the nigga was laying his head and sent Mark and some goons to his house to kill him and his family. I had to send a message to the streets. A bitch was still running shit, and a bitch still had a choke hold on the city. I was the wrong bitch to fuck with.

I sat back down to finish counting money. "That business is handled."

Robert Baptiste

Chapter 31

Shantell

Shit was back to normal. I was getting two hundred thousand from Deloso. I was crushing competition in the city. I was thinking more and more about taking the kids to see their father. Darrell had been calling, but I was ignoring him. I didn't feel right about it after having an abortion. I didn't think I could look at him without guilt overwhelming me. I was hoping that he would get the message and leave me alone. I knew it was cold, but it was the only way I knew to do it.

As I was driving around picking up money. I noticed a black SUV following me. I speed up in an attempt to get to a place with more light. I pulled a 9 mm Glock from under my seat. I would put some bullet holes in their asses, if necessary.

The black SUV stopped beside me. Two federal agents got out of the truck and walked toward me. I put the gun back under the seat.

"Let's go," one agent said.

"Where to?" I asked

The prosecutor rolled down the window." Just get in the truck."

I got in the back next to him as they pulled off.

"It's been a long time since we last conversed."

"I've been busy."

"Yeah, I know, Ms. Bitch. When were you going to tell me that you're getting twenty thousand kilos a month from Deloso?"

"I was getting around to it."

"You want to be smart, huh? I thought this was about getting your husband out of jail?"

"I don't have feelings for my husband no more. Fuck him. He's just my baby daddy. "

"See here, I don't give a shit about you or your drug dealing husband. I put him in prison for thirty years. I don't care if he dies there. I want Deloso. You're going to turn him over to me, or your ass is going down for murder and conspiracy to distribute. I don't care if you get a life sentence and get put in the box next to him."

"You motherfucker. You can't do that. I work for you."

"I'm the government. I do what I want, when I want, to whom I want. If you don't want your mother saddled with your kids, you better pick the right team. Ms. Bitch think carefully about what you want to do. Tell me something in two weeks. "

"You ain't shit."

"When you make a deal with the devil, you always got to pay your debt."

They dropped me off at my car. I drove home.

My head was fucked up. I grabbed a bottle of Patron and hit the shit straight out of the bottle. I found a blunt and lit it, inhaling deeply. What the fuck was I going to do? If I turned on Deloso, he would kill me and my whole family. That was a fact. If I didn't, I was going to jail and would lose my family.

I could see shit clearly now. I knew why Keith couldn't tell. I understood what he meant by it being bigger than his family. You don't know what a person's going through until you in their shoes.

I drank the whole bottle of Patron and smoke two blunts. I fell the fuck out. I woke up with a headache to my ringing phone. I answered, not realizing it was Darrell, but I knew I couldn't keep ignoring him. He deserved better.

"What's up stranger?" he began.

"Nothing."

"Why haven't I heard from you? Why haven't you answered my calls? Did I do something wrong?"

"I've just had a lot on my plate."

"It's everything ok?"

"Yes. No... I don't know. We need to talk in person."

"Okay."

"I'll be there in a couple of days."

"I can't wait to see you."

"Me too."

I still didn't know what I was going to do. I couldn't keep lying to Darrell. He was a good man, and he deserved the truth. I booked a first-class flight to Houston. On the flight, I wondered if this was the right thing to do. What if he was on some bullshit when he found out the truth? Was I willing to take this change if it meant losing him?

Caught Up in the Life

As I got to his house butterflies flooded my stomach. One part of me said I was doing the right thing. The other side said I was a fool. I felt like my heart would break out of my chest.

Robert Baptiste

Chapter 32

Shantell

I knocked on Darrell's door. He answered wearing only boxer-briefs with his dick hanging out. I was instantly turned on, and my train of thought derailed. I grabbed him and started kissing him. He picked me up and carried me to the bedroom. He took off my clothes and threw me on to the bed. He went down and started to eat my pussy out. I was grinding my pussy in his face as I came back to back.

He pushed his dick inside me. I held him tightly, digging my nails into his back as he thrust deeper and harder. He was telling me how much he loved me. As I came back on his dick, I told him I loved him too. He started to shake, shooting all his hot cum in my soaking wet pussy.

I lay back trying to decide if I should tell him, but I fell asleep before making a decision.

The next morning, he brought me breakfast in bed. He leaned over and kissed me. I knew the brother loved me because my breath is banging and in the morning.

"Good morning, beautiful," He smile at me.

I moved the hair out of my face and smiled back. "The breakfast looks good." As I picked up the plate, I saw a small diamond ring. "What's this?"

"Will you marry me?" We've only known one another for a short time, but I'm in love with you. You make me happy. Whatever you're going through, I want to be there for you."

I took a deep breath and lowered my head. Tears started to swell as he raised my head up. "What's wrong?"

"I can't marry you."

"Why not?"

"I've got something I need to tell you."

"What is it?" He looked bewildered.

I took a deep breath. "I'm married. I have two kids. My husband is in federal prison for thirty years. My name is really Shantell Washington."

He looked at me with a confusion still in his eyes, "You've been lying to me this whole time?"

"Yes."

"Why?"

"I never meant for it to go this far. It was just supposed to be fun. You know. You get what you want, and I get what I want. Then we go about our business."

"So, where does this leave me because I'm still in love with you."

"I don't know. I don't want to hurt you. Truly I don't. It wasn't supposed to go this far."

"We all have secrets. I still want to be here for you."

"I need time. I got to figure this out."

"Take all the time you need. I'm here for you."

"So, you're not mad."

"Just a bit confused."

He pulled me close, and we kissed. I stayed a whole week, and we made love the entire time.

***

As I got back to New Orleans, I drove to my mother's house to pick up the kids. Keith Jr. ran up to hug me. Kawine stood back with her arms folded. She looked mad.

"Hey, Kawine," I began.

She walked up and looked me straight in my face. "What's wrong with you?"

"When were you going to tell us our daddy is in jail?"

I was stunned. It fucked me up. She caught me off guard. I couldn't ever come up with a lie. I just swallowed hard. How in the fuck did they find out?

My mother.

I got hot as fish grease. "Y'all get in the car."

I stormed into my mother's kitchen. "Mom, why did you tell them about Keith? It was my job to tell them when I wanted."

"Oh, no. First, I'm you mother. You're my fucking child. Don't try to come into my home like you run shit here. Don't be trying to check me about some bullshit. Second, I didn't tell them shit. Their father called looking for your ass, and they answered the phone. He's been calling for a week now. He talked about how you were supposed to come see him. Your fucking ass should have taken them to see their father. Those kids are twelve and thirteen now."

Damn, I'd forgot. Now I had to hear his mouth.

"I'm sorry," I said.

"I love you too, but I've been telling you to bring your kids to see that man."

***

As I got in the car with a big, fake smile on, I knew I was in for a million questions. I wasn't in love with Keith anymore. Even after I told Darrell, he still wanted to be with me. It made me fall even deeper in love with him. I would always have love for Keith. He was my baby daddy. I would look out for him, but it was time to move on with my life. I had a man who worshipped the ground I walked on and wanted to marry me. I could give him something his wife could not; kids.

When I took the kids to see Keith, I was taking divorce papers. I didn't want to leave Keith at the lowest point of his life. Now that my kids knew where he was, I had the courage to move on.

I looked in the rearview mirror and saw an angry Kawine staring out of the window. She was turning thirteen in a couple of days. I knew how much she loved her father, and that she was mad that I didn't tell her where he was.

"So, Kawine, what do you want for your b-day?"

"I want to go see my daddy."

"I've got a lot of girl stuff planned for us."

"Don't care... I just want to see my daddy."

"Are you sure that's what you want?"

"Yeah."

"I'll take you."

"For real." She smiled.

"Yeah, I'll take you both. '

Even though I didn't love Keith, I couldn't keep them from seeing their father. I also had to choose between Deloso and the government.

Later, I was in the tub when Keith called. I knew I was in for a fight.

"Man, what the fuck is up with you? Why have you been lying about coming to see me?"

"Don't call here with that bullshit."

"Man, you tripping. You must have forgotten who the fuck you're talking to. I'm not that nigga you fucking and sucking out there. It's Keith, bitch."

"I know who you are. I'm bringing the kids next weekend. They want to talk now. I'll talk to you when I bring them. Kawine, your daddy is on the phone. Come get it"

She ran in the bathroom, grabbed the phone, and ran out. At that point, I made my decision. I wasn't giving up my lifestyle for anyone. I knew it was about getting him out of jail at first, but it was bigger than him now.

I was going to stay loyal to Deloso.

The prosecutor would have to give me time. If they had anything on him, they would have already arrested him. They needed me.

Chapter 33

Shantell

I drove over to Beaumont on Saturday morning. The kids were amazed to see the prison.

"Mom, is daddy in there? It looks like a castle."

"Yes, baby, you father's here."

The lady passed the wand over us and escorted us to the visitor's room. About twenty minutes later, he came out. He looked a little older but was still fine and good looking. His hair was cut short with waves. His beard was trimmed right. The khaki uniform was pressed and sat on his shoulders right. I could tell he was back working out. His arms were bigger and more ripped up, and his chest was sitting up nicely in his shirt. His caramel skin had a jail house glow that made me want to take him right then and there.

I never said I wasn't attracted to him. I just was not in love with him no more. He got me wet and turned my pussy on. If he got out tomorrow, I'd still fuck him on the side.

The kids ran up to hug and kiss him. Kawine was hugging him and crying so hard that it made me want to start crying. Jr. did the same thing. Finally, I did as well.

I watched as they played with their father. I was going to give him the divorce papers, but I didn't. Watching him play with them made me remember why I did this in the first place. I got caught up in the drugs, money and the streets. I forgot it was all about getting my love back home. Just watching their faces was enough for me to re-evaluate my decision. I knew what I had to do. If it cost me my life, so be it.

I cringed when I heard Kawine' s question. "Daddy, when you coming home?"

He took a deep breath. "In a little while. In a little while."

"Why can't you leave with us now?"

"Daddy did something bad, so I have to pay for it."

"Okay, but you're going to be home soon, right?"

"Yes, baby girl. I promise."

Keith turned to me. "What did you want to talk to me about?"

I wanted to give him the papers, but my heart said don't. "Nothing. I miss and love you. I can't wait 'til you get home."

"I miss and love you too."

At the end of the visit, we hugged and kissed him some more. I wanted to cry, but I had to be strong for my kids. It didn't matter who I was trying to move on with. I would never find another Keith. My heart knew it.

Darrell was a cool and good man. He would be a good husband, but not for me. When Keith got out of jail. I would cheat on him with Keith and probably leave Darrell.

As I drove back to New Orleans, I thought about how this had affected my kids, especially Kawine. She needed her father. Both of my kids did. Now I had to tell the crew it was over and bust this fool Deloso. I was never telling those hoes that I was working for the Feds the whole time. I was just going to say that we got enough money. Kesha's death would be my excuse.

***

I got everybody to my condo. We sat around talking and passing blunts. "Bitch, I hope this is important. I had some dick lined up," Brittney said.

"Me too," added Jackie.

"It is," I said. I hope you hoes put money for a rainy day. I'm done with the game."

"Bitch, stop playing." Jackie said.

"I'm not playing. Kesha's death made me look at things differently. It made me think about my kids."

"I feel you," Jackie said.

"What do we do with the dope we got left?" Brittney wondered.

"We'll sell it, and that's it. I'll meet with the connect shortly and tell him that I'm done.

"You sure he'll let you go that easy," Brittney said.

"We'll talk about it. I'll be okay, So, everybody's cake is straight?"

We passed the blunt some more and spent the night getting drank, smoking weed, and having a party.

Chapter 34

Shantell

I walked into the prosecutor's office and sat down.

"I see you decided to choose the right team."

"Let get this over with."

"When's the next meeting?"

"Three days. It's at his mansion in Katy."

"Who will attend?"

"Everyone who sells for him."

"Well, we need you to wear a wire."

"No, it'll get me killed. You have to find another way."

"We going to be there."

"Is my husband getting out?"

"We'll take care of it."

Back at home, I thought about what I was doing. Did I really want to put my family in jeopardy to get Keith out of jail? I guess the heart wants what the heart wants. *A bitch will do anything for my husband.*

I smoked a blunt. I knew it was possible my whole family could be killed, but what else could I do? Leave my husband in jail? That was not going to happen.

I noticed my nipples were hurting. Sometimes those motherfuckers get sensitive when I was coming off my period. I had noticed a weight gain in my face and arms. A bitch needed to go on a diet.

On Monday, I found myself at the FBI headquarters in Houston. They put a really small device in my bra.

I couldn't believe I was about to go through this shit. I was really about to put my life on the line. I kissed my mother and kids. I talked to both Keith and Darrell to tell them I loved them.

"Here's a Gucci purse that has a built-in recorder. It's so small that they won't be able to tell it's there," a female agent explained.

Finally, it was time to leave. As I headed toward Katy, I was nervous as fuck. My arrival at the meeting was like always. The guards were patting people down. I was nervous as a motherfucker. They patted me down and checked my purse. That really made me nervous.

I felt like I was going to shit on myself, but they let me by. "Thank you, Jesus," I said under my breath.

I sat down at the table.

Deloso came in carrying his bat. That meant somebody was snitching or stealing his money. Either way, somebody was dead.

He was walking around the table as he talked to us. "Somebody has been talking to the Feds. You know how I feel about that."

Eric walked in the room. As he passed me, a strange look came over his face. Something in my heart told me this shit wasn't going to end well for me.

Deloso made his way toward me. His eyes were as black as midnight. "This time, it's worse than talking to the Feds. They are the Feds."

He raised the bat and hit the heavyset, white man next to me. He turned to me and raised the bat again.

Before he could hit me, the door burst open, and agents were everywhere. Some were sitting at the table. There was a big shoot out. I ducked under the table and watched the bodies fall. Eric fell after being shot in the leg.

Soon it was over. Deloso and Eric were in handcuffs, and most of his team was dead. A few agents had been killed.

The motherfucker was going to kill my ass. Good thing I made the right choice. If not, my motherfucking brains would have been all over the table.

"You're a dead nigga bitch," Deloso said as he was led by me. Death was in his eyes.

I wasn't going to lie. My heart dropped to my ass. I wanted to be strong, but I knew what this motherfucker was capable of. I was worried that this crazy motherfucker was going to send people to kill my family. The crazy part was that Keith would get out of jail and be right in the middle of this shit. Deloso would think Keith put me up to this shit.

I hope Keith never found out.

"You did a good job today." A black agent shook my hand.

"I really hope so."

***

The next day they flew me back to New Orleans and took me to the prosecutor's office. I was only interested in on thing. "When is my husband getting out?"

"About a week. I'm finalizing the paperwork now. We'll put you in witness protection."

"I'm not going into witness nothing. In our agreement, you said my husband would never find out about this. That's the way I want to keep it."

"I understand, but given the circumstances, it's safe for you to go into hiding."

"What about my husband?"

"He can come as well."

"But he can't find out."

"It's your decision, Ms. Washington." "It'll take about a week to process all the paperwork to get you husband out." He turned and looked at me closely. "It looks like you're gaining a little weight."

"Yeah, I want to look good for my husband."

We shook hands. I left the federal building as happy as a kid at Disney World.

Robert Baptiste

Chapter 35

Keith

I was sitting in my cell flipping through my photo album. I thought I heard my name over the speaker, but I brushed it off. I wasn't expecting anything. There were a couple of Washingtons in here. There was nothing for me to do with no visitation on Monday. The lieutenants wouldn't need me for anything.

Lance, my O.G. homeboy from my old projects, bust in my room. I first thought someone was chasing him with a shank, so I grabbed my shank. You had to stay on guard in this motherfucker because shit happened quick in here.

"Man, what's good?" I asked.

"Man, it ain't nothing like that. They're calling for you to pack your shit and roll out." He was breathing hard.

"Man, don't play with me right now."

"I'm serious."

"Keith Washington, report to R&D with your property," the C.O. announced.

"I told you, nigga. Your appeal came through," Lance said.

"That's what I'm talking about," I said, dapping him off. Lance was my guy. He looked out for me when I got here. He gave me a knife and some commissary when I first touched down. Back in the day, I fronted him a couple of keys when he carne home from the state. He caught a Fed beef for ten bricks of heroin and got thirty years. Lance was also a cold -blooded killer.

"My nigga, you're getting a second chance. Don't blow it."

"Man, God is good."

I just took my pictures and mail. I left everything else with Lance. "Nigga, I'm out." I dapped him off again.

I was glad to be leaving this raggedy motherfucker. I had seen a lot of bullshit. Niggas getting stabbed. Niggas getting raped in the showers. A helicopter came every week to carry out a nigga or a cop. They didn't give a fuck who you were. If a nigga felt disrespected, you were getting fuck up. Your paperwork better be right. One thing those niggas in here agreed on was that they hated rats. A rat got fucked up as soon as he got off the bus. You had to roll in a car made up of your homeboys. I rolled with the niggas from New Orleans.

Shit was crazy in here.

"Nigga, be easy out there," Lance said.

"Man, I got you as soon as I get straight."

"Later."

I walked down the sidewalk through a series of gates. In this motherfucker, they got the yard separated because too many people have been killed. Everyone goes to the yard or chow at different times, but shit was still happening. If a motherfucker wanted you, he would find a way to get you."

I knocked on the R&D door. This fine, black chick named Ms. Robertson opened the door. She favored Alicia Keys with a big, round ass.

"Keith Washington?" she asked.

I handed her my ID.

"Come in."

She put me in the holding tank while she checked my paperwork. She had to make sure that I was the person being released. She grabbed some blue jeans, a light blue short-sleeve shirt, and brown boots. I didn't give a fuck as long as I was getting out of here. I swear, I was never coming back to prison. This shit was for the birds. They could keep this shit.

This time had got my mind right. I was done with the drug game. I don't owe nobody shit. I didn't have to worry about motherfuckers trying to kill me or my family because I kept it real and didn't rat.

I wondered if my wife knew I was getting out today. I thought about calling her but decided to surprise her.

I sat in the holding tank waiting for a town driver from camp to take me to the bus station. I was making plans. My ties to the streets were still good. I had a few partners that hadn't been caught. They owed me money because I had helped them get their businesses started. I would take out a small business loan and get my construction business started again.

Caught Up in the Life

***

Shantell

I was waiting at the Beaumont USP parking lot for my husband to be released from prison. I had known about it for the past three days. The prosecutor had told me that everything was a go.

I got so happy I didn't know what to do. I had checked into a hotel in Beaumont the day after I had heard. I had been waiting anxiously for the last two days.

The prosecutor arranged for immediate release, so it looked as if he had won his appeal. He wouldn't know any different. I hadn't told anyone else. I didn't tell the kids about his release. I wanted it to be a surprise.

I cut all my ties to the streets. I got a new cell phone. I gave away almost all my cars and sold my condos. I hadn't told him I had bought the house back. I wanted to surprise him.

I was thinking about moving to Atlanta. I didn't need Keith running into people who liked running their mouths about everyone's business. He didn't need to know what I did while he was in prison.

Brittney moved back to Houston and opened a club. Jackie and Ke'shon were in the process of moving to Atlanta. All those hoes were ten million to the good.

I told Darrell I couldn't divorce my husband. I was sorry for breaking his heart. I hoped he would find someone to love him like he should be loved. He told me that he would be there if I ever needed him.

I sat in the truck, nervous. Butterflies were fluttering in my stomach. I deleted all the pictures of me flossing in the club. The only one I kept was a group shot of me, Brittney, Jackie, Ke'shon and Kesha. I deleted the rest of that shit.

Robert Baptiste

Chapter 36

Shantell

Suddenly there he was in my life again.

I pulled the car up next to him. "You need a ride?"

"Sure do. I'm going your way."

I jumped out of the car kiss him. He hugged me so tight I could barely breathe. "I missed you baby. I'm glad you're coming home."

"Me too. How did you know?"

"They called and told me you were getting out. That you won your appeal. I wanted to surprise you."

"You did that. Where are the kids?"

"I didn't want to tell them, so you could surprise them. Besides, we need some alone time."

"I'm with that."

"I need you to tap this ass."

"Baby, you've picked up some weight."

"I can lose it now that you are home."

We drove to a hotel.

***

Keith

As soon as we got to the hotel room, we started undressing each other. I put her on the bed and began sucking her toes, making my way to her pussy, licking on it a little.

I moved my mouth to her titties, sucking on each one. I made my way back to her pussy licking her clit as she moaned and grinded her pussy in my face. She came back to back.

As I tried to fuck her, she stopped me. "Let me return the favor."

She grabbed my dick and deep throated it like a porn star. It made my toes curl up. I began to shake and cum in her mouth. She got me back hard and climbed on top of me in a reverse cowgirl position. My favorite. She bounced her ass up and down in my face as I thrusted my dick in and out of her warm, wet pussy.

I flipped her over, put her legs over my shoulders and slammed my dick in her. As I felt her nails digging into my back, I explored her mouth with my tongue.

"Fuck, this pussy good."

"It's all yours, baby."

She got into a doggie-style position as I spread her ass cheeks and began eating it like groceries. I slid my dick in her pussy while finger fucking her asshole. She slammed her ass back on me as I slammed in and out of her. We came together, releasing all over each other.

We lay there soaking wet and trying to catch our breath.

Chapter 37

Deloso

I was in my bunk in a maximum-security cell at a federal holding facility. I was here because of that black ass bitch who was working for the Feds. She wanted to get her man out of prison.

I found out that she was working for the Feds through an FBI agent on my payroll. That was how I stayed on top of shit. I put the hit on her using that idiot Blaze. I told him if he took care of the bitch, he could have her spot. He failed to take care of business.

Perhaps, I didn't fully realize how strong she was in New Orleans. I was going to kill her at the meeting, right after finishing that snitching white boy, but things went sideways.

I still couldn't believe Keith made his wife do that. I thought he was solid. I was wrong. That was his plan all along. That motherfucker, Eric, who I let eat for years, took a deal. He testified against me for less time after I made him millions. He wouldn't live to testify. I'd have him killed to send a message. I would kill that bitch and her family too.

They had me in jail, but they hadn't stopped me. I was the cartel boss. They couldn't do this to me. I was fucking Deloso. I was the man in here and in the world. I made sure their families were eating. Now they wanted to take me from my family. No, no, no. I had something for their asses.

My tray slot opened. One of the guards on my payroll gave me a cell phone.

I lived like a king in here. Whatever I wanted, I got. I was eating outside food. I still controlled my cartel from in here. I still had powder on the streets.

I wanted out of this cage. They were going to extradite me to New Orleans soon. In two weeks, they were moving me to an underground federal prison. I needed to get out before the other cartels found out I was in prison. Once they knew I was gone, they'd try to take over my turf. I couldn't have that. I had fought too many wars and spilled too much blood to lose everything.

"Nola."

"Si Jefe"

"Yo necesito give juntes un equipo y saca me de aqui. Yo quieve maten a la rata Eric.

"Esta bien, Jefe."

That snitch thought he would live to get out of prison. His life was over. I just needed to find the bitch and her snitch husband and send them a message.

"I'm not anyone to fuck with."

I was the boss and they were my workers. I'd kill their whole family before doing them. They had to know this would happen. They both saw me do it. I was going to show everybody that I was the man.

The government couldn't protect them. No one could.

I lay back on my bunk. *I might do the work myself.*

***

Shantell

The next day we stayed at the hotel, fucking like horny dogs before returning home. I was anxious for Keith to see the kids. I couldn't wait to see the looks on their faces. My mother was watching them at the house. I bought in Metaire. The kids were out for summer break. I told him to let me go in first.

In the living room, they were watching TV and playing with their phones. My mother was cooking in the kitchen.

I waved for Keith to come in. "Kids, I've got a surprise."

They ran over to me. "What is it? A dog?" Keith Jr. shouted.

"No."

"Then what?"

Keith walked in and they started screaming. Mom came running from the kitchen.

"What the hell is going on?" she started. Then a look of surprise crossed her face. "What in the world?" She hugged him as tight as the kids did. In spite of all the shit she talked, she was happy to see him home.

"Daddy, are you home. For real?" Keith Jr, asked

"Yes."

"For how long?" Kawine asked.

"Forever."

"Good. I didn't want to see you in that place no more," she said.

"You don't have to worry about that. I'm not going anywhere."

"But how?" my mother asked.

"By the grace of the God," he answered.

"I'm glad your home. I missed you,"

"Me too," I said as I kissed him.

"Food is ready. Let us eat," my mother said.

"Sound good," I said. I was so glad I had my family back. All my troubles were behind me. The past could stay the past.

I got a text message on my phone and glanced down.

Black nigga bitch. You think you and your family are safe? You think this is all over? It is just the beginning.

To Be Continued...
Caught Up in The Life 2
Coming Soon

Submission Guideline

Submit the first three chapters of your completed manuscript to ldpsubmissions@gmail.com, subject line: Your book's title. The manuscript must be in a .doc file and sent as an attachment. Document should be in Times New Roman, double spaced and in size 12 font. Also, provide your synopsis and full contact information. If sending multiple submissions, they must each be in a separate email.

Have a story but no way to send it electronically? You can still submit to LDP/Ca$h Presents. Send in the first three chapters, written or typed, of your completed manuscript to:

LDP: Submissions Dept
Po Box 870494
Mesquite, Tx 75187

DO NOT send original manuscript. Must be a duplicate.

Provide your synopsis and a cover letter containing your full contact information.

Thanks for considering LDP and Ca$h Presents.

Caught Up in the Life

Robert Baptiste

By **Aryanna**
THE COST OF LOYALTY **III**
By **Kweli**
CHAINED TO THE STREETS II
By **J-Blunt**
KING OF NEW YORK V
COKE KINGS IV
BORN HEARTLESS IV
By **T.J. Edwards**
GORILLAZ IN THE BAY V
De'Kari
THE STREETS ARE CALLING II
Duquie Wilson
KINGPIN KILLAZ IV
STREET KINGS III
PAID IN BLOOD III
CARTEL KILLAZ IV
Hood Rich
SINS OF A HUSTLA II
ASAD
TRIGGADALE III
Elijah R. Freeman
KINGZ OF THE GAME V
Playa Ray
SLAUGHTER GANG IV
RUTHLESS HEART II
By **Willie Slaughter**
THE HEART OF A SAVAGE II
By **Jibril Williams**
FUK SHYT II

Caught Up in the Life

By Blakk Diamond

THE DOPEMAN'S BODYGAURD II

By Tranay Adams

TRAP GOD II

By Troublesome

YAYO III

A SHOOTER'S AMBITION II

By S. Allen

GHOST MOB

Stilloan Robinson

KINGPIN DREAMS II

By Paper Boi Rari

CREAM

By Yolanda Moore

SON OF A DOPE FIEND II

By Renta

FOREVER GANGSTA II

By Adrian Dulan

LOYALTY AIN'T PROMISED

By Keith Williams

THE PRICE YOU PAY FOR LOVE II

By Destiny Skai

THE LIFE OF A HOOD STAR

By Rashia Wilson

TOE TAGZ II

By Ah'Million

CONFESSIONS OF A GANGSTA II

By Nicholas Lock

PAID IN KARMA II

By **Meesha**

Robert Baptiste

I'M NOTHING WITHOUT HIS LOVE II
By Monet Dragun
CAUGHT UP IN THE LIFE II
By Robert Baptiste

Available Now

RESTRAINING ORDER **I & II**
By **CA$H & Coffee**
LOVE KNOWS NO BOUNDARIES **I II & III**
By **Coffee**
RAISED AS A GOON I, II, III & IV
BRED BY THE SLUMS I, II, III
BLAST FOR ME I & II
ROTTEN TO THE CORE I II III
A BRONX TALE I, II, III
DUFFEL BAG CARTEL I II III
HEARTLESS GOON
A SAVAGE DOPEBOY
HEARTLESS GOON I II III
DRUG LORDS I II III
By **Ghost**
LAY IT DOWN **I & II**
LAST OF A DYING BREED
BLOOD STAINS OF A SHOTTA I & II III
By **Jamaica**
LOYAL TO THE GAME
LOYAL TO THE GAME II
LOYAL TO THE GAME III
LIFE OF SIN I, II III

Caught Up in the Life

By **TJ & Jelissa**
BLOODY COMMAS I & II
SKI MASK CARTEL I II & III
KING OF NEW YORK I II,III IV
RISE TO POWER I II III
COKE KINGS I II III
BORN HEARTLESS I II III
By **T.J. Edwards**
IF LOVING HIM IS WRONG…I & II
LOVE ME EVEN WHEN IT HURTS I II III
By **Jelissa**
WHEN THE STREETS CLAP BACK I & II III
By **Jibril Williams**
A DISTINGUISHED THUG STOLE MY HEART I II & III
LOVE SHOULDN'T HURT I II III IV
RENEGADE BOYS I II III IV
PAID IN KARMA
By **Meesha**
A GANGSTER'S CODE I &, II III
A GANGSTER'S SYN I II III
THE SAVAGE LIFE I II III
CHAINED TO THE STREETS
By **J-Blunt**
PUSH IT TO THE LIMIT
By **Bre' Hayes**
BLOOD OF A BOSS **I, II, III, IV, V**
SHADOWS OF THE GAME
By **Askari**
THE STREETS BLEED MURDER **I, II & III**
THE HEART OF A GANGSTA I II& III

213

Robert Baptiste

By **Jerry Jackson**
CUM FOR ME
CUM FOR ME 2
CUM FOR ME 3
CUM FOR ME 4
CUM FOR ME 5
An **LDP Erotica Collaboration**
BRIDE OF A HUSTLA **I II & II**
THE FETTI GIRLS **I, II& III**
CORRUPTED BY A GANGSTA I, II III, IV
BLINDED BY HIS LOVE
THE PRICE YOU PAY FOR LOVE
By **Destiny Skai**
WHEN A GOOD GIRL GOES BAD
By **Adrienne**
THE COST OF LOYALTY I II
By Kweli
A GANGSTER'S REVENGE **I II III & IV**
THE BOSS MAN'S DAUGHTERS
THE BOSS MAN'S DAUGHTERS II
THE BOSSMAN'S DAUGHTERS III
THE BOSSMAN'S DAUGHTERS IV
THE BOSS MAN'S DAUGHTERS **V**
A SAVAGE LOVE **I & II**
BAE BELONGS TO ME I II
A HUSTLER'S DECEIT I, II, III
WHAT BAD BITCHES DO I, II, III
SOUL OF A MONSTER I II
KILL ZONE
By **Aryanna**

Caught Up in the Life

A KINGPIN'S AMBITON

A KINGPIN'S AMBITION **II**

I MURDER FOR THE DOUGH

By **Ambitious**

TRUE SAVAGE

TRUE SAVAGE II

TRUE SAVAGE **III**

TRUE SAVAGE **IV**

TRUE SAVAGE **V**

TRUE SAVAGE **VI**

DOPE BOY MAGIC I, II

MIDNIGHT CARTEL

By **Chris Green**

A DOPEBOY'S PRAYER

By **Eddie "Wolf" Lee**

THE KING CARTEL **I, II & III**

By **Frank Gresham**

THESE NIGGAS AIN'T LOYAL **I, II & III**

By **Nikki Tee**

GANGSTA SHYT **I II &III**

By **CATO**

THE ULTIMATE BETRAYAL

By **Phoenix**

BOSS'N UP **I , II & III**

By **Royal Nicole**

I LOVE YOU TO DEATH

By Destiny J

I RIDE FOR MY HITTA

I STILL RIDE FOR MY HITTA

By **Misty Holt**

215

Robert Baptiste

LOVE & CHASIN' PAPER

By **Qay Crockett**

TO DIE IN VAIN

SINS OF A HUSTLA

By **ASAD**

BROOKLYN HUSTLAZ

By **Boogsy Morina**

BROOKLYN ON LOCK I & II

By **Sonovia**

GANGSTA CITY

By **Teddy Duke**

A DRUG KING AND HIS DIAMOND I & II III

A DOPEMAN'S RICHES

HER MAN, MINE'S TOO I, II

CASH MONEY HO'S

By Nicole Goosby

TRAPHOUSE KING **I II & III**

KINGPIN KILLAZ I II III

STREET KINGS I II

PAID IN BLOOD **I II**

CARTEL KILLAZ I II III

By **Hood Rich**

LIPSTICK KILLAH **I, II, III**

CRIME OF PASSION I II & III

By **Mimi**

STEADY MOBBN' **I, II, III**

THE STREETS STAINED MY SOUL

By **Marcellus Allen**

WHO SHOT YA **I, II, III**

SON OF A DOPE FIEND

216

Caught Up in the Life

Renta
GORILLAZ IN THE BAY **I II III IV**
DE'KARI
TRIGGADALE I II
Elijah R. Freeman
GOD BLESS THE TRAPPERS I, II, III
THESE SCANDALOUS STREETS I, II, III
FEAR MY GANGSTA I, II, III
THESE STREETS DON'T LOVE NOBODY I, II
BURY ME A G I, II, III, IV, V
A GANGSTA'S EMPIRE I, II, III, IV
THE DOPEMAN'S BODYGAURD
Tranay Adams
THE STREETS ARE CALLING
Duquie Wilson
MARRIED TO A BOSS... I II III
By Destiny Skai & Chris Green
KINGZ OF THE GAME I II III IV
Playa Ray
SLAUGHTER GANG I II III
RUTHLESS HEART
By Willie Slaughter
THE HEART OF A SAVAGE
By Jibril Williams
FUK SHYT
By Blakk Diamond
DON'T F#CK WITH MY HEART I II
By Linnea
ADDICTED TO THE DRAMA I II III
By Jamila

Robert Baptiste

YAYO I II
A SHOOTER'S AMBITION
By S. Allen
TRAP GOD
By Troublesome
FOREVER GANGSTA
By Adrian Dulan
TOE TAGZ
By Ah'Million
KINGPIN DREAMS
By Paper Boi Rari
CONFESSIONS OF A GANGSTA
By Nicholas Lock
I'M NOTHING WITHOUT HIS LOVE
By Monet Dragun
CAUGHT UP IN THE LIFE
By Robert Baptiste

BOOKS BY LDP'S CEO, CA$H

TRUST IN NO MAN

TRUST IN NO MAN 2

TRUST IN NO MAN 3

BONDED BY BLOOD

SHORTY GOT A THUG

THUGS CRY

THUGS CRY 2

THUGS CRY 3

TRUST NO BITCH

TRUST NO BITCH 2

TRUST NO BITCH 3

TIL MY CASKET DROPS

RESTRAINING ORDER

RESTRAINING ORDER 2

IN LOVE WITH A CONVICT

Coming Soon

BONDED BY BLOOD 2

BOW DOWN TO MY GANGSTA

Robert Baptiste

www.ingramcontent.com/pod-product-compliance
Lightning Source LLC
Chambersburg PA
CBHW070455260626
47161CB00004B/1314